Soul Search

Book one of the PIU Series

EK Dobbins

Apellez Dreams Publishing

Illinois, USA

EK Dobbins/Apellez Dreams Publishing
Apellez Dreams Publishing
5343 Belleville Crossing Street
PMB 75
Belleville, IL 62226 www.apellezdreamspublishing.com

Publisher's Note: This is a work of fiction. Names, characters, places, and incidents are a product of the author's imagination. Locales and public names are sometimes used for atmospheric purposes. Any resemblance to actual people, living or dead, or to businesses, companies, events, institutions, or locales is completely coincidental.

Book Layout © 2017 BookDesignTemplates.com

Soul Search/ EK Dobbins. -- 2st ed.
ISBN 979-8-9877350-4-6

Contents

First Day of College

The room is quiet enough to hear the clicking of the instructor's heels as he carefully paces the floor. His piercing eyes scope out the large group of freshman students judiciously. The vast majority of them are focusing anxiety-filled eyes upon the quiz he laid in front of them. One student, in particular, did not adhere to the same worries as her fellows. She glances over all of her short answers for the second time then centers her blue-grey eyes upon the pacing instructor. Her dark shoulder-length hair shifts as she turns her head to continue studying him, noting his sharkskin suit and fin-shaped hairstyle.

She could see that he is human, the same as her, yet he appears to purposefully avoid sunlight in stark contrast to her

Mediterranean tan. She focuses her gaze of curiosity on her fellow students, quietly identifying the many different people from every corner of the known universe. The mask of frustration and confusion plasters every face from the blue skin Larian to the lumpy grey L'phent as they try to answer the advanced questions. Placing her electric pen down, the observer stretches her back and arms to limber up as the minutes tick by nearing the end of the class time.

"Miss Diana Hunter," the teacher's stern voice draws the addressee's attention directly to him. "I'm surprised to see you here at Morstone University, usually Julius sends his kids to Helios Tech in the Orion Galaxy."

"Mr. Murphy," Diana acknowledges with annoyance very evident in her voice. "Why did you give us a pop quiz for Advance Paranormal studies when we are in Basic Paranormal class? Moreover, according to your schedule, we should not be getting a quiz until next week."

"Your disapproval is evident and irrelevant," Murphy sniffs. "However, to appease you, I will give you a blunt explanation. I usually have one or two wise asses in a group of freshmen. I am simply weeding them out to show them that they are not as wise as they think. Many are more like asses. So, which are you?" He snatches up her quiz and grins at her nonchalant look before glancing at the document. His humor leaves him when he sees all one hundred short answer questions complete.

"You are the professor, Mr. Murphy. It is up to you to decide," Diana concludes picking up her backpack as a loud bell sounds in the hall.

"Pens down, leave your quizzes on your desks," Murphy announces to his bewildered students. "Class resumes the day after tomorrow," he quickly turns. "Miss Hunter, I am not done conversing with you."

Diana hesitates in her departure feeling a deep pressure of disapproval enveloping her as she slowly turns to face the teacher. Her fellow students stop briefly but continue to leave as she approaches the professor, places her backpack onto the floor, and meets his gaze. Strange, yet friendly, energy trickles into her causing the tense shoulders to relax. Professor Murphy grins, displaying several artificially sharpened teeth. Diana arches an eyebrow as the feeling of utopia fades as she blocks the teacher's attempt to instill artificial fear within her mind and heart. The move apparently stuns Murphy.

"Professor Murphy, I have other classes that I have to locate on this campus. I do not have time to entertain you," Diana informs.

"You need to change your attitude young lady. With your current one, you may end up in a less desirable position," Murphy hints.

"Are you threatening me, Mr. Murphy?" Diana gives the man a scolding look. "If I'm not mistaken, that is against school policy."

"I know the policy well, Miss Hunter, don't try to school me," Murphy warns then pops his suit coat. "Simply answer my question, why did your uncle decide to send you here instead of his usual venue?"

"I honestly don't think it is any of your business, professor," Diana picks up her backpack again and turns. "However, if you insist on learning the answer, HEL U. was full," she quips walking out of the room without a backward glance.

Chatter fills the light blue halls as students pour into it from various classrooms focusing on their next stop. Diana heads straight out the main entrance into the sunlight and takes out her phone orb. The item starts floating above her hand as a holographic screen lights up to show the order of her classes complete with room number and location. Diana starts walking again, careful to avoid various beings and robotic staff. She heads to a bench to study the map that came with her class schedule. Her next class is Criminal Minds taught by a senior member of the staff, Mrs. Stephanie T. Cummins. The class comes complete with a short novel for a syllabus. After a quick glance through the fifty-page document, Diana decides to go to the library and find a quiet spot to study the information. The sound of French horns echoes as she stands up. She pauses, grumble a little and sits back down, once again retrieving her phone orb to see who is calling.

The holographic image causes Diana to roll her eyes a little before honing in on the caller's blood-red hair and emerald green eyes. Not always are those eyes such an enchanting color, they sometimes turn orange especially when angry. Diana stares at the image and takes a deep breath as if trying to determine if she wants to answer the phone or not. Her voicemail picks up as she makes up her mind causing her to quietly swear. With a couple of more choice words, she listens to the message as she navigates to her contacts and scrolls down until she comes to the name Deloris.

The message concludes as Diana touches the contact to call the woman back. A warm sensation surrounds Diana follow by a slight pressure to her right as if someone is leaning on her shoulder to also look at the hologram. Diana looks up and does a quick scan of her surroundings finding that she is alone upon the bench. A few students are rushing to their destinations, oblivious to her presence. Diana turns her attention back to her phone orb, placing it on her lap. The holographic still image of Deloris is replaced by a miniature version of the woman stretching and then focusing upon the caller.

"Ah, there is our intern. Buna dimineata," the seductive voice of Deloris ooze from the hologram.

"Good Morning, Ma'am. Returning your call as requested," Diana says with a salute.

"It's fine, Diana. You are not on duty. I am just satisfying my curiosity and getting Lawson off my case. He has been asking me for the past hour how your classes are going," Deloris said.

"Well, Basic Paranormal is my first class. The teacher and I already have our disagreements," Diana says while pulling up another window and typing in a few commands. "I am sending you the schedule that I just got this morning, I'm thinking of changing a few of the classes to something that I am more interested in."

"Hmm. Morstone University is notorious for placing students into classes far simpler than they need all to boost their credentials. When they told me that you are going there, I was not very happy about it," Deloris says focusing on the document that is sent to her.

"Uncle Julius is the one footing the bill. I'll have to take it up with him and see if I can transfer to a different school," Diana offers, sitting back and crossing her legs. The sensation of pressure subsides for now.

"I'd have to," Deloris begins but pauses as her eyes light up when she reads the schedule. "Ah, this is fascinating. Your gym teacher is the same one that teaches your Mystical Arts class, Mr. Castaway."

"I don't like that gleam, Deloris. Even as a hologram I can see it very clearly. It usually means that it will be something I'm very uncomfortable with," Diana said cautiously.

"Oh, you'll be fine," Deloris scoffs the worry away. "From what I am reading, Mr. Castaway is a decent mage. Perhaps he can coach you in fostering a relationship with your Aethoes while at the school."

"My Aethoes," Diana grumbles discontentedly.

"Guide, Guardian, Goddess, Mentor, or whatever," Deloris focuses directly upon the intern's eyes. "You are a carbon copy of her and might want to ask why. There may be a reason for it."

"I'm a little too old for imaginary friends, Deloris," Diana folds her arms, her jaw hardening. She feels angry pressure surrounding her briefly but ignores it.

"I hardly think she's imaginary," Deloris scoffs. "She appears to me every so often when you are around. You both are stubborn and resilient, I'm not sure what happened between you two but you have to work it out. Especially if you, Diana, are going to blossom into your full potential."

"I have to go, Deloris. I've got to study the syllabus of my next class," Diana says and picks up her phone orb.

"Understood, but we will have this conversation again and many more times in the coming days," Deloris warns. "I will see you tomorrow at the office." The phone orb goes silent.

"Unfortunately," Diana grumbles as she stands up, placing her device in her backpack.

The campus is mostly clear by the time the conversation is over. Only a handful of the students are wondering about the campus to get their bearings. Diana shifts her pack to her back mumbling in discontent. A large signpost next to the bench points the way towards her destination, the library. With a nod, she moseys in the direction of the short structure, ignoring many of the stares she receives from a variety of students. A young man drops his history book as she passes him. He shakes out of his stupor and scrambles to pick it up. The wind opens the book and turns to the Ancient Greek history chapter. It stops on the page with a picture of a statue of Artemis. The young man gawks at the picture then he looks up at the departing woman.

A happy breeze toys with Diana's hair as she stops in front of her destination. She brushes back a stray strand and analyzes the building. It is a single-story; unlike the rest of the campus with a cornerstone boasting that it is nearly three thousand years old. The building is a half-block wide with the length twice as much. The pitched roof and strong columns remind Diana of an old temple of some sort. She grins to herself, of course, it is; a temple of learning. The doors to the building open automatically as she approaches them, their silent operation is almost eerie. She steps into the entrance and pauses to wait for the glass edifices to slide back together. Once the doors close, a red light pops on to scan the intruder. The robot guard then casts a green light to welcome the student to the facility.

The smell of dust and old books invades the woman's senses soon after she got the green light. Diana sneezes, bringing attention from those that already occupy the library with a number of them scowling disapprovingly at her. Taking the silent hint, she quietly makes her way into the main part of the library. Volumes of shelves and books stack several feet high, reach the ceiling and provide a stairway to higher shelves for the smaller beings of the universe. Corridors made from the bookcases are marked with every subject from every available source to include intergalactic institutions. Diana wanders the entire library and notes that all available seating is full of her fellow students either studying or sleeping before their next classes. Diana takes another glance around then decides to cross the main archway towards the museum.

"Well, this is pretty," Diana whispers.

The dark halls of the library open up into the bright and clear galleries of the museum. Sunlight stream in from the wall as well as the ceiling of windows that enclose the artifacts. Replicas of ancient statues stand proudly in the light of the halls. Diana observes that the replicas are Ancient Greek statues. Holographic signs above three halls point the way towards the Norse, Egyptian and Aligon history. Diana remembers going to a museum that is actually dedicated to the alien residences of Earth. She had seen that many of their statues reflected those upon Earth. Diana glances at her watch and sees she had wasted at least forty-five minutes wondering the library in an attempt to find a seat. She calculates that she still has at least an hour to go and decides to camp in the Greek exhibit until her next class. Diana takes one more step into the space.

The light suddenly goes from bright and cheery to an off blue, chilly illumination. All the statues turn and watch her with their eyes glowing to life. The effects cause Diana to stop in her tracks and hesitantly glance behind her to see the tables are all still occupied. The light shifts back to normal as she slowly turns to face the direction she travels. All the statues have returned to the normal position, the lights above flicker as birds fly overhead.

"I'll have to see what the cafeteria is serving as breakfast," Diana concludes.

A few people start to trickle into the museum, following Diana's example of finding an unoccupied spot to relax before class. Diana shifts her backpack and starts walking past the different statues, greeting them one by one. The first statue she sees is the tall and proud edifice of Athena. Decked out in her golden robe and helm, she is a beacon especially when sunlight bounces off of her. Diana acknowledges the rest of the major and a few minor deities before she rounds a corner to find an empty spot underneath the statue of Artemis. Diana once again shifts her pack a little as her face twists a slightly in discontent then finally shrugs and walks to the bench and places her pack down.

The footsteps of the museum's patron echo as Diana stands in front of the statue. She places her hands upon her hip and tilts her head back to study the larger than life replica of the Ancient Greek Goddess. Artemis stands with bow ready, an arrow drawn to her cheek. The wind is blowing towards her in the carving, her hair pushback, toga pressed against her form. A mask of determination dominates her facial features, her eyes glaring into those of her unseen enemy.

Seven figures lay dead at her feet with the assumption that whatever she battles had killed them. Diana takes a walk around the statue to examine it. She notes that the aim of the giant bow is actually towards the Criminal History hall of the museum. Diana once again stands in front of the statue with a nod. The features of the ancient figurine are very familiar to her. She sees them every time she looks in the mirror. Diana has no problem posing for artwork; however, this statue was carved many thousands of years before her birth.

Diana notices the autograph of the artist, Homer Achilles. She pulls out her phone orb from her backpack to use a holographic application to scan the signature and look him up. A curious look crosses her features when she reads that he was a blind artist that carved many of the statues now featured in museums around the universe. In a recorded interview Homer claims that he could see the subjects that he carves.

Diana flips through all of the pictures of each statue Homer Achilles carved and feels as if she is pouring over a family album, each statue of a deity resembles one family member or other. After going through the album, Diana decides it is time to get back to her studies. She has to read the small novel provided by Ms. Cummins for her next class. She pulls out her wireless earpiece and stuffs it in place as she sits down upon the bench to listen and read about her class.

The shadows of the statues slowly shift as time marches by coupled by various visitors drifting in and out of the museum. Many of them pause to openly stare at the woman and statue combo. Diana ignores the people as she twists her features in confusion. She sits up and scratches her head as if to figure out a puzzle. A strong and friendly energy trickles down from the statue as Diana shifts her position, determination upon her face to understand the very cryptic messages the teacher has for her students. Her movements frighten those that are admiring the statue. Diana pays no mind to them as they hurry away, muttering their embarrassment. She pulls one leg under her form and lets the other one dangle to the floor. Her intense concentration is interrupted upon hearing someone clear their throat.

"Diana A. Hunter," a young woman catches the attention of the addressee. "Is the 'A' short for Artemis."

Diana slowly looks up to see who greets her. The woman smiles brightly back at the less than humored freshman. Her amber eyes are laughing in the light of the room. Diana knows that this woman is an athlete. They have raced several times around the track during their high school competitions. Since then, this one-time rival athlete has developed a larger natural feminine chest. Her light brown complexion is kissed with a blush of red, brunette hair braid and falls past her shoulders.

"It might," Diana places her phone orb away, recognizing her antagonist. "So now what, Raquel?" She stands and picks up her backpack as she speaks to the six-foot three-inch woman.

"Hey, easy. We are rivals on the track not off of it. You're still my little friend. I just want to welcome you to Morstone U.," Raquel chuckles. "Try not to be too serious, it's bad for you. For a minute there I thought the look carved on the statue drizzled down to you." she grins a little when Diana relaxes.

"I was trying to figure out Ms. Cummins's biography," Diana said.

"Oh, God no," Raquel interrupts, as she rolls her eyes. "That woman is on the brink of insanity. I hope you are seeking guidance from your look alike."

"That bad, huh?" Diana shifts her backpack. "Unfortunately, I still need to go. Do you know where the Expo building is at?"

"I've been here for a year. Of course I do," Raquel grins brightly. "I can show you. If you can keep up." With that, Raquel turns and runs down the corridor that leads to Criminal History.

"I'm a seven-time track and field champion," Diana scoffs and shoulders her bag. "Keep up indeed."

The sounds of the remaining visitors soften as Diana takes a couple of steps after her competitor. Her eyes flash slightly indicating that she is drawing from a very strong source of energy as her pace increases. It only takes a moment for Diana to see the back of Raquel as they both run past a museum guide bot and several visitors. The robot sounds off a whistle, calling out to the duo that running is not allowed and they should slow down. The racing pair ignores the warnings and whistles as they turn a corner, avoiding a couple fascinated by an ancient painting. Diana pulls up to run right next to Raquel, issuing a taunt or two as they near the egress of the building. They reach the doors and throw them open as they exit the building before the guide bot could catch up to them. The structure is quickly a small space on the horizon behind them.

The campus is once again teeming with people forcing Diana to slow down a little to avoid them and give Raquel a slight lead. The sophomore is quick to take advantage of the freshman's slowdown and begins to bob and weave through the crowd with expert ease as the freshman following closely. A herd of L'phant students rumbles down the lane, filling at least half of the walk area. Diana sees the large grey beings first and makes a wide berth left to avoid getting tangled up in an enormous group. Raquel doesn't pay any attention to them as she glances behind to see how close the freshman was. She turns back around and almost collides with one of the smallest members of the L'phant heard. Raquel unleashes colorful language as she slows down considerably to dodge through the group. Members of the herd snort and make angry sounds at Raquel for interrupting their routine.

Diana keeps pace with Raquel on the side of the group to keep watch over her as she makes her way through the herd. The L'phants begin to spread out prompting Diana to knuckle down and escalate her pace to get past the large beings before they converge on the entire lane. She develops a small lead as she passed the head-bull of the L'phants and barely dodges his angry trunk as he strikes out at her. Diana then hears her challenger not too far behind her and reins in her speed to allow Raquel to once again take the lead.

An intimidating structure, a half-sphere looms into view and seems to be the very building they are heading to. Made from black glass, it is easy to believe the sphere is modeled after an eclipse and dwarf many of the dorms on campus. The large neon lights on the side scroll across to highlight events that take place at the center. Its name, Expo, proudly is etched upon the glass and shadowed the fraternity house that stood right up against it.

Diana grins and leans into her run as another strong surge of energy fills her body causing her stride to increase. In a matter of a few short seconds, she is neck and neck with Raquel. Diana's body tingles as her eyes once again gleamed, focusing intensely upon the finish line. She barely hears Raquel's unhinged words and ignores the woman's struggle to keep up as Diana effortlessly expands her lead. She dodges a few straggling students then jumps to clear a small ditch and finally stops at the entrance of the building. Diana paces a little to bring down her heart rate and calm her breathing. The rush of energy lowers as she continues to move, falling back to where she mysteriously stores it. Diana finally catches her breath and observes as Raquel takes the bridge over the ditch, slowing for the traffic of students going to and from various locations. The taller woman arrives, panting heavily as she falls to her knees in an effort to catch her breath.

"I swear that you are some sort of enhanced human," Raquel breathes. "Or even an Aligon. But, hell, you left even the Aligons in the dust when our high school competed in the Intergalactic Olympic Games."

"I barely left them in the dust," Diana recalls as she holds out a hand. Raquel accepts the help to her feet. "I took a blood test. I am human, just not a genetically enhanced human."

"You need to take another one," Raquel insists. The bell rings signifying the change of classes. "Op! Got to go! Cummins's class is to the left," she says hurrying back toward the library.

"Thanks," Diana calls and quickly enters the Expo Building.

The interior of the Expo Building is in constant twilight thanks to the window treatment of the atrium. A cafeteria greets

Diana along with a few dozen students sitting down to eat lunch. She ponders the menu then rubs her stomach, contemplating. She decides not to eat the food, remembering the strange effects breakfast had upon her with the statues earlier. Diana concentrates on getting to class even though she is already a little late. The light dims then darkens considerably in an attempt to swallow Diana as she makes her way to her destination.

Diana feels her senses go on high alert as she pauses at the sudden appearance of the outline of a young woman floating in the corner. The woman's hair is disheveled; a torn and tattered gown barely hides her figure, eyes nothing more than blank slates. The lines going down her face indicate she was crying, perhaps for an eternity. Diana takes an instinctive step back as the woman glides over to her and appears to speak. The freshman listens as intensely as she can but did not hear the message the specter is conveying. The ghost teeters back and forth a little bit, her face clouding up as tears start to flow again. The spirit places her hands upon her face, covering her eyes as she turns to float down the hall rapidly.

The ghost suddenly disappears in a brilliant flash. Diana creeps down the hall, searching about to take in details of her surroundings. The straight hall offers no other features except the door that is at the end. Large and made from an ancient tree, it bears the marks of many students that passed this way in the form of carved graffiti. A large golden plaque in the very center of the door proudly displays the name Ms. Cummins, Ph.D. Diana frowns and turns in place to see if she can locate the exact area that the ghost disappeared. A flash of golden light briefly illuminations up the dark hall but does not keep the bleakness at bay. That brief light is then followed by a deep maroon light coming from up the hall couple with a wave of dangerous energy. Diana feels something urge her to get into the room as she turns and reaches for the door. The old door swings open just as she is about to touch the handle causing Diana to jump back. She is greeted by an elderly lady with pen up hair and a crooked nose. Her skin leathered with age as the majority of her body is covered by a long black dress decorated with white ruffles. Overly large glasses sit upon the bridge of her nose magnifying her mysterious blue eyes.

"Don't just stand there gawking, come on in," the old woman huffs.

"Ms. Cummins I presume," Diana addresses.

"Yes, I am," the woman agrees, "and you are Diana Hunter. Is it by chance a play on words, I wonder? Would your family really be saying that you are Diana, Goddess of the Hunt? And what do you hunt?"

"I, like several million little girls, was named after her," Diana crosses her arms across her chest. "Why do you target me for such interrogations?"

"Because you look like more than just a simple name," Ms. Cummins shrugs. "If you bother to look in the mirror, you would know why I asked such a question. One rule is to never deny the obvious, it will only add to the discomfort of your interrogation," she stepped to one side. "Your seat is in the front of the class, Miss Hunter. There are only five students now. It might be less by the end of the day. Are you woman enough to stand the class, Criminal Minds, or are you a coward?"

"Are you woman enough to handle your own medicine?" Diana retorts, a trickle of agitation in her words.

"That goes without question since I am the master and you are the student," Ms. Cummins said without flinching. "Take your seat, Miss. Hunter. The hall is drafty."

Ms. Cummins walks away, leaving Diana standing in the doorway steaming at the words of the elderly woman. Diana senses something next to her still insisting on her getting into the room. Diana ignores the nagging feeling as she contemplates why she is taking this class. A force gently pushes upon her prompting a grumble from the young woman as she follows the professor into the classroom.

The door quietly closes itself as Diana makes her way to her seat ignoring the stares from her fellow students. Ms. Cummins focuses her eyes on her new prey and grins brightly at her, the gesture is not meant to provide comfort nor did it. Diana meets the woman's gaze, unfazed until the teacher starts talking. Diana then rolls her eyes as the lecture centers not only on her but the rules and objectives of the class.

The agony of the first day of class finally lifts as the last bell of the day rings. Nearly all the students shout joyfully, grateful for making it through the initial day of classes. Diana ambles to the Robotic hover-cab stop, unhurried. She speaks a greeting to one of her fellow classmates. He ignores her as he runs to get to the parking lot where his vehicle awaits. The daytime students continue their rapid pace to the exit in a very unorderly fashion.

Their replacements, the evening and night class students, are just as eager to get into the university. Diana arrives at her destination and leans against the post, watching the traffic jam to exit the campus. Horns of all types and varying degrees honk with the results of receiving a variety of responses to include a slew of cuss words and gestures. Diana focuses on the distant horizon, her mind quietly drifting back to her last class. Slightly unsatisfied with the class, she focuses on the ghost and energies appear in front of her prior to entering the classroom.

Diana closes her eyes as she recalls the brief meeting of the ghost woman and the details of the interaction. The strange golden light next to her as she approached the door did not faze her as much as the dark maroon energies from the path leading back to the entrance of the Expo building. Diana concentrates on her memory of the maroon light and tries to condense it down only to fail in the exercise. She opens her eyes and grumbles a little; perhaps she is still irritated by the antics of the last class, specifically the teacher's words and actions.

Diana recalls that Ms. Cummins likes playing games and uses them to teach. Diana focuses her eyes upon the hues of the evening sky, recalling the objective of the class, Criminal Minds, is to actually think like a criminal. Diana figures the old woman will give her a headache twice a week, especially if Ms. Cummins continues to address her as the 'Goddess of the Hunt' then follows on her question of 'What do you hunt?'.

Diana churns over the information about the class over and over and concludes that the only thing she may possibly get out of Ms. Cummins class is the fact that she will learn to outfox a criminal. Then again, the P.I.U.'s specialty is ghosts and mystical justice more so than 'normal' criminal activity. Diana decides to simply drop that class in favor of something more aligned with her chosen career. She plans to look at the schedule as soon as she gets home and hopes it is not too late to change the class.

The continual blend of horns and voices fill the air as Diana takes out her earbud and connects to her phone orb. The holograms illuminate brightly as she shifts through different applications to find the hover-taxi app. A small cryptic keyboard appears to allow her to type in the information and confirm the cost as well as the locations of both the pick-up and destination addresses. The orb then changes colors and makes a polite beep as it confirms the information is sent and accepted by the taxi. A small icon of a rolling cartoon car replaces the application screen as Diana closes the app. The orb goes silent as she places it into her backpack.

"Diana," Raquel sings causing the addressee to cringe from the sound.

"Now what madness is going on?" Diana mumbles as she turns to face the intruder.

"I'm glad you're still here. You remember Laurie," Raquel smiles as she introduces the woman that stands with her.

Diana focuses on the blonde bombshell that playful curls a tip of her golden tentacles around a finger. The woman smirks at Diana as if remembering a past event that caused the freshman some anxiety. Diana frowns a little, sensing something not quite right with Laurie as if she changed the year or two that separate their classes. A grin of triumph plaster Laurie's pretty face as her bright blue eyes are met with Diana's blue-grey.

"Yes, I remember you," Diana admits. "You were the cheerleader captain with an ill-mannered boyfriend."

"I'll admit we had our ups and downs," Laurie sniffs. "However, he is now totally loyal to me and we are engaged," she casually flicks her hand to show the large diamond engagement ring.

"Congratulations, I am sure you and Wyliam will be happy," Diana said with very little fanfare.

"Our wedding is in a few months and Raquel is one of my bridesmaids," Laurie continues.

"I'm glad," Diana remarks then is distracted by a chime on her phone orb. She pulls it out to look at the screen with a slight frown.

"There is a party to celebrate, but not tonight," Raquel explains. "Tonight the Alpha Norma Sigma fraternity is hosting the First Night Party. Everybody on campus is invited."

"Are we going to see you there?" Laurie inquires with a smirk.

"No, I can't," Diana answers as she feels a cold wind go down her spine. "I will have to pass this round. One, I don't live on campus and secondly, I now have an appointment to speak to the one funding this education. I don't want to be late for that."

"See, I told you she wouldn't go. She's still nothing more than a little kid," Laurie boasts to Raquel.

"Are you sure, Diana?" Raquel besieges. "You're no longer in high school, time to socialize like an adult." A yellow hovercab quietly stops in front of the waiting station.

"Yea, I'm positive, maybe next year," Diana reiterates and opens the door to the cab, sitting in the backseat.

The screen in front of Diana illuminates brilliantly allowing her to enter her credentials and confirm her address. The form is then replaced by a friendly male cartoon figure smiling brightly. A short, cheesy, animation of the taxi in motion plays then disappears as a street map came up. A red blip indicates the current address of Morstone University, a green one was the destination. The hover-cab hums to life and lifts off the ground. Air from the engine blows out, pressing on the clothing of Raquel and Laurie, forcing them to step back to allow the door to close.

Diana watches the two shrink in size via the side mirror as they cab lifts and direct itself to a less crowded exit. Her curiosity peeks when she witnesses Raquel appear to cower a little from something Laurie says as she walks away. Diana sits back and stares at the screen, watching the blip inch closer and closer to the destination as she ponders the interaction between the two.

The evening sun hangs a little lower in the sky by the time Diana reaches her apartment. The hover-cab approaches the building slowly and assures it docks correctly before letting the door open. Diana eases out of the cab and stretches. She picks up her backpack as she walks towards the three-story building. Diana pauses to take in a few of the details, noting that the building has columns on both sides and the windows are all universal. The left side resembles the right side and the whole building is painted antique white. The color makes it stand out among the other apartment buildings nearby. Diana approaches the door as the hover-cab whisks away.

"A good perk to being assigned to the P.I.U. is that you get your own apartment," Diana speaks quietly as she removes her card from her backpack. "The downside is that you are on call 24/7."

The entrance hall greets the weary student with a bright and cheery feeling. Diana checks her mailbox then head straight up to her third-floor apartment. The door opens at her approach, welcoming her to a beautiful and orderly interior. Two bedrooms and just as many baths, it is a sizable apartment. The door closes and locks as Diana wanders into the kitchen, depositing her backpack upon the couch in the process.

Humming a delightful tune, she puts together her dinner and brings it to the living room. Diana sits down on the couch, pulling her datapad out. The screen lights up as she props it up onto a stand in front of her. A picture of her uncle pops up on the screen causing Diana to nod as she slurps her noodles, he is right on time. She gives a verbal command to answer the phone call.

"Good evening Uncle Julius," Diana addresses, stirring her meal with a spoon. "I received your message and was about to give you a call."

"I hope so," Julius agrees. "I was a little worried that you were going to a certain frat event this evening. It's all over the news, the First Night Party."

"I opted out of the party," Diana informs. "I just did not feel comfortable going." She stuffs a spoonful of her meal into her mouth.

"According to the news, it is a bunch of bachelors taking advantage of the freshmen class," Julius waves it away. "Glad you have good Hunter sense, staying out of trouble. So, tell me about your day." The man on the screen leans forward, his fingers touching at the tips as he peers into the camera.

"I met two of my teachers, ran into an old track rival who was once a good friend and ran into a former cheerleader captain from high school," Diana sums it up. "Professor Murphy knows you and asks why I was not sent to Helios U."

"A misunderstanding with a few of the board members prevents it this year. I will see about next year," Julius informs. "It was about your brother."

"Oh, Okay. That answers my next question," Diana finishes off her meal. "Ms. Cummins is annoying at best. She kept addressing me as the 'Goddess of the Hunt' and presses the question, 'What do you hunt?'"

"I've read reports on Ms. Cummins and even researched her V.I. character. She is a strange but knowledgeable teacher," Julius said. "I have to agree with her on the question she asks of you. What is it that you hunt, Miss. Artemis?" He smiles warmly when he sees his niece roll her eyes.

"Anyway, uncle," Diana quips. "I've got to get going. There is a little homework I want to get done to include the posed question. If I don't answer it, she is going to drive me crazy with it. That is her promise."

"Take caution about a hasty answer, Diana," Julius warns. "Ms. Cummins is crafty enough to know when you rush an answer and when you take your time. You should answer it at the right time, in the right place." He leans back a little. "I saw your schedule, you are off tomorrow. Are you visiting?"

"I will make an effort to. I might have to bring Deloris along though," Diana admits. "I'm still an intern and Lawson wants me to learn as much as I can from her."

"Deloris," Julius grins slowly, rolling the woman's name off of his tongue. "Then I look forward to the meeting."

"Of course, Uncle. Good night," Diana said and hangs up the phone. She stands to take her dishes to the kitchen.

The datapad chimes again as Diana completes cleaning up her kitchen prompting the young woman to swear a little as she dries her hands and goes over to see what the alert is about. The title 'New and Exciting' flashes across the screen drawing in her curiosity. She touches the display and a video pops up proudly displaying the Museum of Past Modern History and its latest exhibit, Amamet, devourer of souls, apparently open to the public for the first time this century.

A wave of shock then anger fills the room prompting Diana to shutter and turn off the datapad and news yet the strong feeling did not go away. Diana paces back and forth as the feelings linger then decides to sit down and rub her temples a little. Several minutes will pass before the wave of anger finally dissipates as whatever was in the apartment departs. Diana takes a deep breath in and out then head towards her bedroom to prepare for the night. She has a feeling that it is going to be a long day tomorrow starting with Deloris.

CHAPTER TWO

First Night

The fires of the setting sun become lost among the beauty of the forested landscape. She sits within a grassy knoll admiring a new bow, pleased with her work. The sudden appearance of several frightened deer brings her to her feet. She notches an arrow to her new bow and points in the direction the deer fled from. The smell of smoke soon wafts in her direction followed by the unmistakable crackling of a fire. Cussing, she switches hands with her bow and makes a fist to slam into the ground harshly. Taking a step back, she allows the newly formed spring to geyser forth and directs it to the advancing flame.

The fire hisses and gurgles in anger as it collapses, consolidating to become a strange creature. She once again notches an arrow to her bow and pulls back as the creature pushes through the tree line. The beast lets out a strange bellow and snorts. The archer temporarily lowers her bow as she stares at the intruder, never has she seen anything like it until today. It has the head of an alligator, shoulders and forelegs of a great cat, with the rear end of a hippopotamus. The beast centers its gaze upon the woman, lifts its maul, and lowers it with the bellow of flames shooting directly at the observer.

The archer drops a bit of foul language as she leaps high into the air then pulls and lets go of her arrow at the attacker. The flames go underneath the woman and the arrow sails directly to the beast slamming into the nose. She releases a second arrow aimed at the creature's left eye. The missile strikes true, blinding the beast and causing it to howl in pain. The archer lands back on her feet and readies a third arrow only for the ground to shake violently as the creature stomps around toppling trees and causing a massive canyon to open.

The woman cries out in surprise as she falls into the canyon but manages to grab the edge with her free hand. The creature lumbers over, looking down and opens its mouth to swallow her whole. The woman let's go and falls down into the canyon. She flips around loads and fires her bow upwards at the beast burying the arrow in the chin of the beast. Attached to the arrow is a mystical rope that she grabs and holds onto. Her body slams into the side of the canyon, causing great pain. She continues to hold the rope as the beast above thrashes back and forth to shake her free. She quickly climbs the rope reaching the top in record speed and once again stands on solid ground. She did not see the beast's rear end until it hits her sending her flying into a tree then sliding to the ground. Shaking her head, the archer looks up in time to move as the beast snaps at her, biting through the tree she once laid against. She realizes that her hands are free and sees that her new bow is at the feet of her attacker. The beast turns steps on the bow and breaks it with a satisfying gurgle coming from its throat.

"Diana," the creature grunts and charges for the archer.

The archer glares at the beast once again, jumps over and lands behind it only for the ground to give way. Air whistles in her ears before she meets the jarring coldness of a wooden floor. She looks up and around, her name continuously called. Diana blinks at the four white walls of her bedroom. Two doors also greet her, one leading to the bathroom, the other to the rest of the apartment. The bed and other furniture are carved from artificial wood in the shape of trees.

Diana stumbles slightly as she tries to stand to find the source of the voice calling out to her. She finally gets her senses clear enough to notice the sheets are wrapped around her, figuring that she and the inanimate objects became entangled during her nightmare. Diana turns to the window to see the crack of dawn approaching. She quickly looks down at her attire as sleepiness finally starts to clear her mind. She is still wearing red and yellow pajamas. Her ears once again hone in on the mechanical voice that repeats her name in rapid succession.

"Oh, shut up!" Diana snaps at the alarm clock as she slaps it.

The alarm clock flies from the top of the dresser and into a wall, destroying as soon as it hits the obstruction. The pieces of it slowly fall to the ground then evaporate on contact. Diana watches in shock as the destruction appears in slow motion to her. She pulls back her shaking hand, barely noting the rattle of her breath as she tries to breathe and think through what just happened.

Movement to her left alerts Diana to quickly turn and face the threat. She hesitates when she sees that it is just her reflection staring back at her. She carefully approaches the mirror and touches the area near her face, staring into her eyes. Instead of her usual color, they were a brilliant and semi glowing blue-green. A golden image in the mirror catches Diana's attention and causes her to take a step from the mirror. The image solidifies enough to make out a few very familiar features to the young woman. Diana swears and turns to the area the alleged specter is standing in the room, she sees nothing. Looking back at the mirror, Diana sees the golden specter tilt her head and looks up slightly.

"Buna dimineata, Diana," a friendly, familiar voice speaks from behind.

Diana freezes when she hears the words and stares into the mirror. The golden image did not say anything that she could see. In fact, the specter seems to be staring up then following the invisible intruder down. The hair on the back of Diana's neck stands up as she slowly turns. The first glance of the invader causes Diana to drop an unkind word as she completely whips around then take three steps back, nearly toppling over the mirror. Her face of shock turns into one of outrage as Deloris finishes levitating to the ground.

The senior officer is wearing her P.I.U. uniform which is all black. A sweater hugs her feminine form with a golden badge clinging just above her left breast. Her eyes are also dark but lightened back up when she finally stands upon the ground. The right corner of her lush red lips ticks up slowly, revealing one of two very sharp pointed teeth.

"Good, you are awake. We have a case," Deloris said.

"Deloris!" Diana snaps angrily.

"Scuza," Deloris questions as she arches an eyebrow.

"Ok," Diana takes a deep breath in order to calm her reaction and nerves. "Why didn't you just call me?"

"I was already in the neighborhood and this is much faster," Deloris informs with a warning in her tone of voice. "Get dressed; we are to meet Lawson at Morstone U."

"Morstone? What happened?" Diana asks.

"Get dressed," Deloris repeats. "We have precious little time."

"At least tell me how you got past the security bots and into my apartment," Diana insists.

The room's temperature warms up slightly as the two watch each other intensely. The small amount of silence is enough for Deloris to hear the intern's heart rate. It increases slightly then levels out as the agitated young woman awaits her answer. A soft glow starts to surround Diana as many nearby electronics either dim or go blank altogether. The golden 'specter' approaches Diana and stands next to the her, facing the vampire with a slightly scolding look. Deloris snorts as if humored when she decides to answer the question else something might explode. The last thing she wants is for Diana to detonate.

"As senior officer of the P.I.U., I am able to invade the homes of lesser officers in case of emergency," Deloris said in brief. "Get into uniform so we can depart for Morstone. Lawson is waiting. You will learn more when we get there."

"Fine," Diana grumbles as she turns to go into the bathroom to get dressed.

Deloris quietly decides to ignore the lack of protocol from the intern for now. After all, Diana did awaken in a high alert state from whatever she dreamt about. Deloris turns and leaves the bedroom to sit upon the couch and await the intern. In the bathroom, Diana grumbles to herself and splashes cold water upon her face to complete her wake up. She looks up into the large mirror over the sink to see she is alone and that her eyes have finally returned to normal.

She pulls on a pair of blue khaki pants then yawns mightily as she tugs on her black tee-shirt. She stifles another yawn as she puts her light blue jacket on; making sure her name badge is still attached. Diana stretches a little and shakes her head in order to shake off the last of her sleepiness as she leaves the room and travels to the living room and the awaiting senior officer. Deloris looks up from her reading when she hears Diana enter the room.

"I must admit, you do look the part of a full-on officer," Deloris admires as she stands. "However, you still have a lot to learn, to include contact with your Aethoes."

"My Aethoes," Diana repeats with a bit of contempt to her words.

The floor and ceiling appear to blend as Diana finds herself lifted up off the ground and then crashes back down onto her stomach. All air seems to leave her lungs as she feels a great pressure upon her entire being. She lets out a sound of frustration and pushes up, managing to only get her torso up then get slam once again to the ground.

Deloris confidently leans on the arm of the couch and watches the intern struggle a little more then turns her attention to the golden figure with an outstretched hand standing at the window. Diana lets out a sound of agitation and punches her fists against the floor causing a pulse of energy to wave over it and hit all the electronics in her apartment. Every piece of furniture in the building starts to admit a low and threatening hum.

"Deloris," Diana manages in angry notes.

"I'm not the one doing it," Deloris admits calmly as she cleans her shades and places them on. "It appears you are not very receptive to the idea just yet. Even though your Aethoes is currently holding you down with a simple thought. So, to avoid any massacres before we reach Lawson, I will refrain from the subject for now. We will revisit this in the future."

"How do I get up?" Diana growls.

"You are the one to dictate that," Deloris said.

Deloris shakes her head a little when she sees Diana once again try to stand up. The intern manages to get her knees under her only to be lifted once again and flattened out, this time on her back. The barely seen form of Artemis folded her arms and continued to focus upon her mortal doppelgänger. Diana sputters angrily as she manages to get onto her stomach and then became immobile all together. Deloris checks her watch and frowns at the time; they have wasted several precious minutes.

"Unfortunately, you are not learning your lesson and I am afraid you never will in this manner. There is really no reason why your Aethoes should keep you held down. It does not serve the purpose she intends it to." Deloris offers. Artemis appears to think about the words before she simply turns away and disappears.

"Deloris, I told you," Diana snarls as she once again gets her hands under her body and pushes up strongly. Instead of meeting the same force, she battled for five minutes or more, she ends up turning herself over. "What...? You finally let me go?"

"Not I," Deloris once again reiterates. "The hover-cab is waiting outside for us. We should get to Morstone U. within the hour, traffic is light for right now."

Diana slowly gets to her feet as Deloris walks out of the apartment. The young woman looks around to see no one else is there. With a slight frown, Diana follows the senior officer out and closes the door, locking it soundly. She sees several of her neighbors out of their homes to look around, apparently something shook the building and they are looking for the source. Diana waves to a few of the people she knows and continues to the outside, unable to stop and chat. Diana exits the building and quickly enters the awaiting hover-cab. The door closes and the vehicle lifts off, quickly taking the streets to the nearest highway exit to Morstone.

The duo arrives at their destination nearly an hour later. The Alpha Norma Sigma fraternity house is built in the style of an old Victorian Tudor. Its upkeep is very apparent as it is the best-looking building on the campus. Stained glass with various depictions occupies the second level of the structure. The first-floor windows are tinted to keep prying eyes out. It sports two visible towers with two hidden ones directly behind. Gray and white in color, it stands out against its neighbor the Expo building. The front door of the frat house is a bright red with the name of the fraternity proudly etched in its frame.

Flashing lights from the media and safety robots annoy at least one resident of the hover-cab. Deloris hisses quietly then makes a low, barely audible growl as she adjusts her shades to protect her sensitive eyes from the glaring radiance as she sits back to relax. Diana, on the other hand, is glued to the window in fascination from the amount of living and mechanical crew that the hover-cab has to press through to reach the destination. She spots a tall and lean yet elderly man with a head and scraggly beard full of salt and pepper hair. His uniform is similar to those worn by the passengers and hugs his frame well. Diana watches as the man places a stick of gum in his mouth, turns, and swaggers toward the frat house as their vehicle finally makes it through and park near the spot he just left.

"Looks like Lawson either did not see us or wants us to meet him in the frat house," Deloris said as the vehicle comes to a stop. "Let's get out of this circus, shall we?"

"Any way we can avoid them altogether?" Diana requests.

"You'll have to get used to it, especially as a member of the P.I.U.," Deloris informs unapologetically as she opens the door.

The media crowds around as Diana and Deloris exit the hover-cab. Hundreds of voices blast out a million questions all vying for the two ladies' attention. Deloris makes a displeased sound and starts walking, an invisible force pushes against various media personalities as she continues her way. Diana wisely decides to stay with her supervisor in order to get to the frat house without being stopped by the aggressive media.

A large security-bot lights up and levitates as the women approach. Green LEDs turn red and glow menacingly upon the mechanical being. The approaching officers stop with Deloris folding her arms. She makes sure the intern is standing next to her as a bright blue light shoots out from the chest of the massive machine and scans them both thoroughly. Diana flinches a little when the light hit her eyes. The scanning light goes out as the security bot LEDs turn green moving to one side to allow the door to open and the cleared officers to enter the scene.

The officers walk past the threshold of the stately building and glances behind when the door closes with a loud thump. Deloris takes off her shades as Diana gawk at the condition of the room they have entered into. The interior of the frat house boasts ancient floral wallpaper currently stained with age and unrecognizable liquids in the foyer. The large room may have held a grandfather clock at one time, the pieces of which are scattered throughout the area. An old overturned chair sits near the wall with many cuts and abrasions befitting of an old warrior.

Off to the left of the front door is the entrance to the kitchen, to the right of is a large stairway leading upstairs. Above the kitchen door frame is a mural of a mermaid perhaps painted during the party. The carpet of the foyer may have once been a lush red now it has a variety of dark stains of dirt and other things grounded into it. The rails of the large spiral staircase are carved to resemble a snake slithering down the head of which is above the first step. There is an open door under the staircase that reveals the coats of the fraternity brothers and a heap of discarded clothing. The ceiling, also painted, has a mural of various mythological creatures and ancient deities intermingled. Among the mural painting and symbols is a chandelier that dangles down. The light fixture groans as it is heavy with the weight of discarded feminine underwear.

"Well, there's enough up there to open a minor lingerie store," Deloris comments.

"Might have a major brand, we didn't investigate the closet yet," Lawson agrees, his voice a little gruff as he turns to face his officers. "It was the First Night Party. A night of drinking, ladies, and dancing in togas or with lampshades, your choice."

"And you know this how," Deloris inquires.

"All over the news, might have gone to one or two in my life-time. But not this one," Lawson admits.

"That's not…whoa," Diana places her hands on either side of her head as she is still trying to take it all in. "What happened?"

"A girl attending this party was found presumably dead in one of the rooms upstairs," Lawson recaps. "Reports, however, state that she still has a slight heartbeat. She was rushed to campus hospital. They have her on life-support right now. I was sent her pictures."

"That sounds more like a case for the regular police department, not the P.I.U.," Deloris said. "Why are we involved?"

"I received an anonymous phone call about this place and party about a half-hour ago," Lawson admits. "Usually, I ignore such things but this time the caller was very persistent so I figured we would just come on down."

"I was invited to the First Night Party by a couple of fellow students," Diana frowns.

"Glad you didn't go," Lawson nods to the intern. "Would have been hell trying to explain the events to your uncle."

"Or they might have been avoided," Deloris counters.

Diana did not hear the conversation between Lawson and Deloris as her attention goes to the discarded chair near the wall. She approaches the item carefully noting that the piece of furniture's floral design rivaled that of the wall. It is overturned and missing one leg with more stains than the rug. Diana assumes that the dried stains are blood from the various residences of the fraternity hall or the partygoers. A glint of gold catches her eye as it beckons from the hole left by the missing leg. Diana carefully tilts the chair until the gold necklace tumbles out onto the floor. She picks it up curiously and sees that it is a small Egyptian Ankh. She reaches and touches the centerpiece and is interrupted when she hears voices coming from in front of her.

Diana looks up, stifles her immediate reaction as she takes a step back from the images of the wallpaper. The large flowers of the design now resemble screaming women all of whom were vying for her attention. The movement of the mouths and sounds of the screaming causes Diana to move further back, holding her ears as she shakes her head. As suddenly as it started the noise and screams disappear. Diana lowers her hands from her ears. The intern shakes her head to clear it and once again takes a look at the jewelry she clutches.

"Let me see what you have there," Deloris requests sternly causing the intern to jump and turn. "You know better than to pick up things during an investigation. This could get you fired or worse, jail time." She holds out her hand.

"The regular police have already done their search and secured the scene before my arrival. They took everything that they needed or wanted for their investigation then left. The security is in place until we are done, at my request. Our time is limited so let's see if we have a case," Lawson admits as he starts up the stairs leading to the second level.

Diana returns her attention back to the wall as Lawson disappears into the gloom of the stairwell. Deloris watches him leave as she speaks to the intern about the necklace. She does not get an answer and turns to the young woman to see that Diana's focus is on the wall. The intern jumps when her senior officer calls her name again. Diana explains what she is looking at. Deloris goes over to the wall and touches the paper feeling that is just old with perhaps a few layers behind.

Undaunted, she takes a step back and tunes into her bloodlust, briefly, taking a second look at the wallpaper. She is now able to see a variety of bloodstains decorating the flowers on the wall. She also senses that they are being watched by a very unfriendly entity. Lawson calls back downstairs to his officers prompting Deloris to close her eyes and relax returning to a calm state. Muttering a few words about impatience, Deloris hands the necklace back to Diana as she follows the man upstairs. Diana places the jewelry in her pocket, takes a second glance at the wallpaper, then heads towards the stairs. As she puts her foot on the first tread, Diana's instincts kick in and she whips around to face the room.

"Who's there?" Diana demands. A ghostly figure barely shimmies into light in response causing the young woman to stare a moment. "Who were you? You seem a little familiar."

The ghost moves to the left slowly then back to the right as it seems to study Diana intensely. The specter's intense white color changes to a deep and dangerous maroon as it centers in and charges forward. Diana takes a deep breath in, faces the stairs once more and bolts as a powerful force urges her escapement. The ghost rushes after her only to hit an invisible barrier harshly then wails in anger as it disappears. Diana barely notices that the ghost is not chasing her as she reaches the top of the staircase in record time. The darkened halls of the upstairs stretch out in three directions as Diana searches for either Lawson or Deloris.

A high-pitched noise penetrates her hearing causing Diana to wince in pain as the darkness appears to twist on her. A strong, gentle force pushes her in one of the directions and urges her to run as fast as she could. Diana instinctively obeys the request heading down the hall quickly. Voices moan and scream in her ears as to floor buckles under her feet.

Diana trips, falls, returns to her feet and continues her way ignoring the skeletal hand that is trying to keep her down. She is able to make out the outlines of her companions and calls to them. Deloris whips around when she senses danger and prepares for a confrontation as rushing feet near. Lawson also turns when he hears his name being called and notices Diana approaching them rapidly. Deloris is about to scold the intern when she notices Diana slide to a halt and turns to face the direction she traveled.

"What's wrong?" Deloris demands.

"I don't know. Something or someone, perhaps a ghost," Diana explains. "It looks familiar but I couldn't tell you who. It charged at me. Instinct told me to run so I did."

"I see no ghosts," Deloris scowls, glancing around.

"And I ain't afraid of them," Lawson quips. "Diana, ghosts are part of our jurisdiction. Perhaps it wanted to tell you something."

"If her instincts told her to run, it is good she listened," Deloris counters. "In Diana's case, it is not instinct that urges her to act at all times."

"You're going to give me a headache with an explanation if I pose the obvious question, aren't you?" Lawson focuses on the vampiress with a knowing scowl. Deloris simply smiles in response. "Right, I'll stick with what we have going on now and ask later. Diana, stay close to us."

"Yes sir," Diana agrees.

The wooden floors of the hall echo with their footsteps as the trio finally reaches the room that is the actual crime scene. A robot greets them with a blip as it acknowledges their approach and opens the door. The mechanical being then salutes before it levitates past the P.I.U officers, heading down the hall in order to leave the house. Diana enters the room first and pauses taking in the immaculate condition of the room.

A large king-size canopy bed is the focal point of the bedroom followed by an impressively large chest leaning against one of the walls. A river of fresh rose petals covers the floor from the doorway all the way to the bed and has the appearance of being untouched. She finishes her scan by taking in the very clean marble floor and a squat nightstand next to the king-size bed. Diana walks into the room completely, careful not to disturb the rose petals, as she studies the bed. She sees that it has been made as if somebody took care to keep the place very clean. The only exception is an indent in the comforter where the victim once laid.

Lawson comes into the room next and watches as Diana bends down and picks up a rose petal to study it. He goes over to the canopy bed and pulls out a small camera to take a few extra pictures at different angles then bends down and looks straight at the bed as if searching for clues. Outside the room, Deloris stays back and looks over the door frame, keenly aware that she is missing something. She reaches over and gently touch the wood feeling carvings but does not see them.

Making a curious sound, Deloris carefully brings up her bloodlust once again and places her shades upon her eyes. She sees not only are there symbols but they are a combination of Egyptian hieroglyphics and Ancient Greek lettering. The color of the glow from the symbols ranged from deep reds to light purples and even a few blues. Deloris calms down her bloodlust again and removes her shades as she frowns at her discovery briefly. She enters the room to take in what is going on inside.

"Something is odd about these," Diana says about the rose petal. "It feels strange."

"Let me see what you have," Deloris requests, accepting the petal and holds it up against the light. "There is a symbol meticulously drawn upon it. This symbol resembles what I saw on the door. Who in their right mind knows all of this in today's world?"

"What kind of symbols are you talking about," Lawson asks.

"They are a combination of Egyptian and ancient Greek symbols that even I am pressed to interpret," Deloris admits.

"I can name at least five people just off the top of my head that would know that type of information," Lawson boasts. "I have at least one of them on speed dial if we like to talk to her."

"I can understand some ancient Greek letters but not Egyptian," Diana admits. "But I'd have to see them in order to read them."

"Well, there you go," Lawson says triumphantly.

"Something about this feels very unreal," Diana said as she approaches the Commissioner. "Sir, can I see the pictures from the initial investigation?"

"Yep, I have the right here. I took a look at them but did not see anything out of the ordinary. Then again, my talents are not as paranormal as yours." Lawson said.

Lawson hands a datapad to the intern before he goes over to the chest of drawers and starts opening each one to go through the contents inside. Deloris looks over Diana's shoulder as the intern taps the screen to bring up the pictures from the initial investigation. The room is in the same condition as they have found it which is not surprising except there is a body on the bed. The victim has clothing on although it looks as if someone has dressed her.

Diana makes a small sound of curiosity as she swipes to the next picture to see a close-up of the victim's face. She is an attractive girl, her eyes are wide and stare blankly at the wall with a mask of terror upon her face. Diana frowns at the eyes but turns to the next picture showing the victim's entire body once again. Deloris quietly points out that the victim's skin is blushed in the picture, she is not pale like a corpse. The senior officer also notes that the nails are still intact and that the wrists are slightly bruised as if she had chains upon her. Diana acknowledges the bruising then once again swipes back to the face and zooms in on the eyes. Instead of pupils as expected, they see that the eyes are nothing more than blank whites.

"Lawson, are you sure this victim is human?" Deloris gently takes the datapad to study the eyes of the victim.

"Is she blind?" Diana adds to the inquiry.

"DNA tests show that she is human. What medical records I could get indicate that she is not blind either," Lawson informs.

"They also show that she was not sexually assaulted. She is still a virgin."

"That explains the rose petals. But not the symbols on them," Deloris hands the datapad back to Diana.

Lawson completes his search of the large chest and turns his attention to the closet, opening the door. He taps on the walls listening for hollow spots. He does not immediately find it on the wall thus turns his attention to the floor as a commotion outside garners Deloris's attention. She goes over to one of two windows only to come face-to-face with the enormous black dome of the Expo building. Its highly polished glass reflects the frat house pristine and seems to rest upon the lower roof.

The early morning sky barely takes over the dome. Deloris decides to switch windows to look out once again. From her new vantage point, she sees that there is a tower previously undetected and nearly hidden by the Expo dome. Deloris calls for Diana to come take a look outside with her. The young woman turns the datapad off, places it in her pocket, and starts for the window until she feels eyes on her. Bit by bit, she faces the entrance of the room and tilts her head when she notices a young man staring at her intensely. Diana scans the intruder and her expression goes from curiosity to perturbed.

"You are aware that you are trespassing on a police investigation, sir," Diana said sternly to the stranger.

"The rest of the police have left for the night, determining that the victim passed by natural causes," the young man said, his voice smooth to the ears. "I am surprised to see you in my room."

Lawson closes the closet door and turns to the entrance to study the interloper. The young man's blonde hair reaches down to his shoulder. He is currently wearing a dark green pants suit with a light purple shirt underneath. Although the clothing said nothing about his style sense, they did hide his large strong shoulders. Light brown eyes dance with humor as he continues to focus on the young lady in the room. Deloris turns from her vantage point to watch as the scene unfolds. Her senses tell her that the young man, with terrible fashion sense, is actually a very powerful magic user of sorts.

"We are finishing up our investigation," Lawson informs. "You are the one that found the girl, state your identity."

"Of course, I'm Beryl," the young man introduces. "I'm the newly elected leader of the Alpha Norma Sigma fraternity. I will admit I was not expecting a young woman in my room but when I found her, she was unresponsive. I called the emergency line as soon as I knew something was wrong."

"Did you put her clothes back on," Diana asks, catching the attention of the young man with her question.

"Why of course," Beryl grins fully at the questioner. "I wanted her to maintain some sort of modesty. I try to respect all of my ladies." A small gleam goes across his eyes as he meets Diana's gaze.

"I am glad you respect the ladies, Beryl," Diana acknowledges. "However, do not try that trick again. It's annoying."

"What?" Beryl blinks in surprise.

"Not weak-minded as you like, eh Beryl?" Deloris chuckles. "Oh, don't look to me, I did nothing to fort your plan. Tell me what really happened?" She casually reaches out with her mind and finds resistance from her intended victim.

"It is like I said. I found her in my room," Beryl reiterates. This time he is not as friendly. "Please leave before I call my lawyers."

"Very well," Lawson relents. "Ladies, shall we?"

"Yes sir," Diana and Deloris answers.

The sound of voices downstairs echoes throughout the house as Diana approach Lawson and returns as datapad to him with a salute. She then walks past the Commissioner and exits the room ignoring the vibes she receives from Beryl. As she enters the hall, Diana notices that it is much lighter than when they first walked down.

There is no trace of ghosts or entities of any sort. Diana glances over her shoulder to see that Deloris has also entered the hall and has a slight state of shock on her features. The senior officer turns around and scans the door touching the wood and taking note that there are no longer any symbols within the grain. Diana bends down and looks straight across the hall to see that there is no buckling or imperfections to indicate something has broken through it.

"What is going on?" Diana muses.

"This house has been here for a very long time. I have no doubts that it is haunted," Deloris said. "There is a very, very un-friendly entity that has taken up residence here. It is hiding right now since Beryl returned."

"I do not like this house," Diana muses as she stands back up. "Something about it is eerily familiar. Although I have never stepped foot into it."

Diana frowns thoughtfully leading the way down the hall and ultimately down the steps. She hesitates at the bottom when she sees the fraternity brothers have all returned and are cleaning the house. A number of them are righting the furniture as well as repairing and cleaning it. Deloris recognizes a large group of the frat brothers are human with the exception of maybe a few weaker aliens from further in the Milky Way galaxy. Diana steps fully into the room bringing all cleaning to a standstill, briefly. One of the frat brothers grins brightly at the young lady as she makes an abrupt left and exits the fraternity house.

Deloris takes note of the man quickly processes that he is actually an illegal vampire. He has been one for a number of years now and it is too late to punish either him or the vampire that turned him. The male vampire's gaze finally tears from the door to the woman staring at him from the stairs. His eyes widen as he takes a step back and a very short breath in. Deloris simply rolled her shoulders glances behind her to see Lawson is following then walks out the building with the Commissioner.

The morning sun blinds both Deloris and Lawson briefly upon their exit of the building. Deloris makes a little hiss to show her displeasure at the sudden bright light. She grumbles a little as she puts her shades back on to protect her sensitive eyes. She notices the intern stretching and yawning in the morning light. Diana's attention goes back to the frat house as she once again removes the necklace from her pocket.

The transparent form of Artemis stands with the young woman as they both seem to contemplate the situation. Diana turns the necklace over to study the relic, seeing that there are various ancient writing etched into the golden centerpiece. Lawson pulls out a device and hits a button to summon the hovercars. A short distance away two of them beep to acknowledge the command and slowly make the trip towards the trio. Diana decides to ignore the cars as she heads towards the library on campus. Artemis turns and walks with her as she frowns in curiosity.

"Where are you headed?" Lawson asks the young woman.

"Sir, I am going to the library to research the Alpha Norma Sigma fraternity and the origins of this necklace," Diana faces the man and salutes with her answer. "Research should not take any more than a few minutes."

"Wait for me," Deloris chimes. "I think your Aethoes is also curious."

"Deloris," Diana shakes her head. "I told you yesterday that I am too old for imaginary friends."

"And I informed you the same day that she is not imaginary," Deloris retorts in a matter-of-fact voice. "She is standing next to you and is very upset at your words. Especially since you did experience a few of her abilities firsthand earlier this morning. Did you forget so soon?"

"Time out," Lawson interrupts, "both of you. What is going on?" He watches them face him.

"Diana has a need to connect to her Aethoes to understand her full capability," Deloris explains in short. "So far, she is stubbornly denying them."

"Just because I somehow look like Artemis does not mean I have got the same ability," Diana retorts, a bit of resentment in her tone.

"True. But you have something. A connection," Deloris said with a tinge of agitation in her words. "Why else would she be staying so close to you?"

"Ok wait," Lawson holds his head and shakes it a little. "This is what I am hearing. Diana, you have some abilities that you are not developing and Deloris has sensed this and is trying to bring them out." He holds up a hand to keep the two silent. "Diana, as an intern you still have to listen to your mentors. Deloris is the only mentor of the P.I.U. since we were formed less than a week ago." He turns towards Deloris. "You, my fine vampire lady, need to become a wee bit more human and try not to pressure the girl so much."

"Hmm...very well," Deloris relaxes her shoulders. "Let us get through this research, and we will talk about your Aethoes at a later time."

"Unavoidable I suppose," Diana grumbles. "Alright, we can talk later." She assured. Deloris cracks a half-smile when the young woman agrees with her.

"Good, all is well now and the hovercars are here," Lawson nods at the black and white hovering sedans. "I'm going straight to the office. I want you two there by noon."

"Yes sir," both women salute their commissioner as he gets into the back of a car.

The door on the car closes and the vehicle rises up onto a cushion of air. The red and blue lights flash yet the sirens remain silent as the vehicle glides to the exit of the campus. Diana quietly contemplates Lawson's departure and suddenly wishes that he had taken Deloris with him. The young woman mumbles a few thoughts under her breath as she once again starts walking towards the library. Deloris simply smiles, walking in silence next to the intern. The hovercar soundlessly parks next to the library building.

The library doors are locked at first until Diana shows her student badge. The doors open allowing entry into the foyer. The security robot to scan the two visitors. A single light waves over Deloris twice to make sure she belongs on the campus, stopping once it hit her P.I.U. badge. Two beeps exit the mechanical being as it opens the door to allow the visitors to enter. Diana walks into the library and heads straight for the holographic data tower to log in and start her quick research. Deloris takes off her shades and scans the area finding it odd that the library is so small and cluttered. She also sees and senses a number of unsettled spirits due to the long history of the building.

"Is this it? The building is bigger on the outside. What's in the rest of it?" Deloris asks.

"The rest of the building is host to the school's museum, and offices for the librarian and museum curator." Diana summarizes. "The museum has the biggest footprint. I've already found what this Egyptian Ankh means. But the symbols are far different than the examples online."

"Perhaps if we find out whom it belongs to, we can find out what those symbols may mean," Deloris said.

"I'm not sure I have that access. I will see if I can hack into the school database archives to find the information," Diana said as her eyes continue to be glued to the hologram of the data tower.

The lights in the library hum to life one at a time, preparing to open the doors for the day. Deloris sits down in one of many semi-comfortable chairs and waits as Diana continues her dataquest. The senior officer watches the various ghosts of the library dutifully avoid the young woman and her Aethoes. Deloris also sees Artemis try to talk to Diana about the jewelry. For the most part, Diana either ignores her Aethoes or does not hear what is being said.

The young woman tenses a little every once in a while when she feels something brush against her. Deloris watches the interaction of the two carefully as she places her hand on her knee and ponders the connection between them. To the vampiress, the connection seems very weak, but it is still enough for Diana to draw energies and power from Artemis without realizing it.

Deloris carefully considers the situation and concludes that she has to assist the intern in the connection. She is only concerned as to how she is going to do so. A book floats over towards the vampire catching her by surprise. Deloris stares that it momentarily then turns back to the data tower to see Artemis nod to her. The senior officer quietly takes the book and reads the cover.

"Guided meditation...I see," Deloris stands. "Diana, did you find anything?"

"No, it won't let me in," Diana gripes a little. "Something does not seem right."

"Perhaps the museum will offer us more clues," Deloris motions to the darkened archway. "A good stretch will also help your mind. Have you any questions about the victim from the First Night Party?"

"My only question is; why are her eyes blank," Diana asks. "The information we have does not add up to what I saw in those pictures."

"The eyes are the window to the soul," Deloris assures. "Lawson did mention that she is not blind." The hall darkens a little then lightens as they pass under the archway and into the atrium of the museum.

"So, as a wild theory, we can say her soul has been stolen?" Diana said with a slight frown. "Do we go to the hospital to make sure? How will we?"

"That could be one of your abilities," Deloris offers. "Do you have an understanding of your current capabilities?"

"I can thwart mind control tactics," Diana admits with a bit of pride, "learned that as a young girl. For some reason, I can run like the wind. I excel in track and field competitions." She pauses when they come across Artemis' statue, looks up and smiles a little. "I guess that's one or two things I have in common with her. I remember pretending to be her as a little girl. I had all kinds of fun. Then something dramatic happened... and I was not greatly fond of her since then." Her smile slowly fades as memories haunt her.

"I know you do not want to hear this, but your Aethoes also appears to have memories of the dramatic event. She seems sad when you mention it," Deloris folds her arms and leans against a column.

"You actually see something," Diana confronts her coworker.

"Of course," Deloris said nonchalantly. "I've had a lot of time to develop my psychological and metaphysical awareness. What I see is that you, Diana, are a carbon copy of your Aethoes. Same as the statue behind you."

"I look like her, that's no surprise," Diana waves the comment away. "Melody looks like Athena. Sometimes I swear she acts like her too."

"I'm sure," Deloris chuckles. "Well, let's see. Your Aethoes is wearing a toga, shortened to the knees. I believe that is good for long strides in running. She has a nice powerful-looking bow across her back complete with a quiver. Those arrows are deadly. She also has a silver circle around her forehead holding back a lush mane of golden hair. A little longer than you like, eh?" She addresses the transparent version of her intern.

"How do I know she is here and you're not making this…" Diana starts her complaint but ends up jumping when she feels something touch her arm and her name whisper in her mind.

"That is her. She is also behind the pressure that held you to the floor in your apartment before we left," Deloris laughs at the reaction. "Would you like to see for yourself, what I see?" The halls go silent as Diana carefully considers the offer. Deloris simply brushes her sleeve a little as she concentrates on the intern.

"You're not going to let this go until I agree, eh?" Diana makes a face of discontent.

"You know me well," Deloris said.

"Fine," Diana grumbles in defeat. "What do I do?"

"Sit on the bench and relax," Deloris instructs. "Allow my mind to unlock the chains that you placed upon yours. I will not harm you. Your uncle is too damn close to Hades for me to do anything foolish."

"According to him, if something drastic happens to me he'd simply bring me back to life and scold me," Diana quips as she sits down. "He is always serious so I was never sure how to take his comments."

"You'll find out if you perish," Deloris assures as she approaches the young woman and stands just a few feet from her. "Gaze into my eyes, and relax your mind. Breathe in and out, deeply and slowly in a meditative rhythm. Quiet your concerns."

Deloris's voice echoes in the room as she continues to weave her magic. The familiar scene of the museum starts to turn fuzzy to Diana as she squints to focus on both the words and her surroundings. Feeling the resistance, Deloris scolds the young woman gently and once again tells her to relax. Diana mumbles a little in frustration then actually takes the advice of her senior officer and sits back a little. Moments later Diana detects a very bright golden light actually sitting next to her. Diana blinks a few times so that the room can once again come into focus. She sees Deloris standing in front of her with a triumphant look about her features.

Diana tilts her head questioningly until the bright light once again invades her senses. She turns and locks eyes with the blue-green orbs of the lady that sits next to her. Diana stares at her intensely and reaches out to touch what she believes is simply a mirror. However, the reflection does not move the same way. Diana touches the arm of Artemis then jumps up and back when she notices that the golden woman's arm is solid. Diana backs up several paces until she is standing next to Deloris. The golden glow around Artemis fades completely as she appears flesh and blood, the same as Diana.

"I...Whoa," Diana stutters as she stares at the woman. "This...this is real? No, can't be...." She shakes her head in disbelief.

"I told you," Deloris said triumphantly. "That your Aethoes was as real as you and me."

"I..." Diana stampers.

Deloris is stunned when she hears Diana's heart rate increase threefold as fear began to overtake the young woman's breathing pattern. Diana's eyes once again lock with those of Artemis and the young woman takes a few more steps back. The adrenaline in Diana's body begins to flood as Artemis is replaced briefly by a giant ball of flames in the intern's eyes. Diana shakes her head violently as the seated deity once again starts to glow, this time it is silver. Diana's body also takes on the silver sheen as Artemis senses something wrong and Diana once again starts moving away.

"No...I don't want....no.... Just Go Away!" Diana turns and flees out of the room.

Deloris watches in stark amazement not expecting the reaction received. She again wonders what has happened between the two. Artemis is laser-focused on the hall that Diana disappeared down as she gets to her feet and follows after her, fading into obscurity as she does. Deloris figures that it is best to locate Diana as the young woman is very upset now and could hurt herself or even worst, kill herself. Not one to take the chance, the senior officer also goes down the hall to track down the young woman and hopefully find her prior to something bad happening.

CHAPTER THREE

Unleashed Energy

Powerful energy plummets Diana during her headlong run through the long halls of the museum. Several voices whisper her name with one sounding above the others calling to her desperately to slow down or stop. Instead of obeying the request, she increases her speed as bolts of energy course through her muscles. Diana barely takes time to open the museum doors as she bursts forth from the structure. Tears stream back as she holds her ears and quickly cuts around the corner heading towards the school's square. Diana feels the heat from the flames that accompany the unlocked memories.

The course of her mad dash soon takes her into the path of several resident students exiting their dormitories to start their day of classes. A lot of the scholars either cry out in surprise or otherwise express their displeasure when Diana nearly collides with them. She ignores the calls as she dodges through the crowd instinctively. Up ahead, Raquel exits her dorm as Diana quickly approaches it.

The sophomore swears and jumps back to allow the stream of color to pass her. She hesitates in shouting obscenities to the runner when she realizes that the blur is actually the freshman that she greeted yesterday. Raquel calls out to Diana then unleashes words that would make her mother blush as she drops her books and runs after the freshman, quickly kicking up to speed.

The internal voice within Diana soon becomes nothing more than a soft buzzing as the power surge she once felt starts to pull back. At the same time, Raquel musters a second wind to increase her stride coming within striking range of the one she pursues. Moments later Diana feels two different people grabbing her shoulder and pulls back. The combination effectively puts a stop to her mad dash to nowhere.

Diana falls to her knees, panting heavily as her body starts to tremble uncontrollably. She looks up briefly to see the clear sky. To her mind's eye, a ball of flame once again careens towards her suddenly. Diana tries to stand up but finds it impossible, something strong is holding her down. She shakes her head to try and free herself from both the memory and the obstruction. Raquel takes a couple of deep breaths and calms her own breathing then kneels down next to the freshman to check on her.

"Diana, what happened? What's wrong?" Raquel asks with some concern. "Are you alright? Speak to me girl."

"I..." Diana stammers. "I don't..."

"Easy, calm down," Raquel coaxes, "and breathe."

An ear-piercing sound penetrates Diana's hearing causing her to hold her head as her body convulses a little. Surges of energy course through her causing the young woman to cry out in pain. Raquel reaches out and touches Diana only to pull back when she gets an electric shock. The sophomore stands and takes a step back from the trembling woman, unsure if she is going to explode. Diana punches the ground creating a small hole as she fights to gain control of the energies within and surrounding her. She feels an arm go around her shoulder and hears buzzing which somehow soothes the raging powers.

Diana's breathing soon slows down to a quivering pace as the heat fades from around her. Deloris arrives and stays back briefly as she witnesses Artemis kneeling next to Diana. Raquel is standing off to the side, unaware of the Aethoes's presence as well as that of the vampiress. The senior officer takes in the distance between the library and their final destination admirably.

"Well, she got further than what I thought," Deloris said. "She is still upset I see."

"Stay back, vamp," Raquel warns as she faces the intruder. "Leave her alone."

"Else what?" Deloris asks with great humor to her words. "That almost sounded like a threat. You need to work on it. Diana had a paranormal encounter that she was not truly expecting. She is otherwise fine."

"No thanks to you I see," Raquel accuses. Deloris snorts.

"I've little time or patience to deal with you, cur," Deloris dismisses and turns her attention to the intern. "Diana, we have to calm your nerves, get you something to eat, and meet Lawson at the station."

A small crowd of students including several Alpha Norma Sigma fraternity brothers gather around the trio to watch the interaction. Deloris takes a step closer to Diana only to be physically pushed back by Raquel as she provides another warning to the vampire. The altercation actually causes Deloris to take a single step back in surprise. The senior officer's features turn from annoyance to outright deadly. In a flash, Deloris has her hand around Raquel's throat and lifts the sophomore off the ground holding her at arm's length. Raquel gags and struggles to breathe as she feels the stranglehold that the vampire has on her grow tighter.

Deloris is about to bring the sophomore closer in order to draw blood, stopping when a golden arrow buzzes between her and her prey. The vampire glances to one side to see that Artemis has reloaded and is now taking aim at Deloris. The senior officer lets out a little snarl then once again focuses on her prey, dropping her and turning away. Raquel crumbles to the ground rubbing her neck. Artemis carefully lowers her bow and puts her arrow away, for now.

"You are lucky this time, girl," Deloris said to the sophomore.

The vampiress ignores Raquel's coughing as she carefully approaches the intern. Diana manages to go from kneeling to sitting upon the ground as her breathing starts to become more normal. She has her head lowered and eyes close to concentrate on keeping herself conscious. Her hair and clothing are plastered to her body due to the enormous amount of perspiration pouring from her body. Artemis sits on the ground in front of Diana, patiently. Deloris carefully gets to one knee so that she can touch the intern's head. The senior officer frowns a little when she detects that a strong force has also awakened within the young woman.

"Diana, are you alright now?" Deloris inquires gently.

"Deloris, what did you do to me?" Diana whispers. "Please, make it stop."

"All I did was unlock the door so that you can see and hear your Aethoes," Deloris assures. "Like it or not, she is somehow linked to you."

"Is there a way to unlink it?" Diana inquires looking up.

"Do you see her now? She is sitting right in front of you," Deloris said.

"No," Diana admits as she scans the area.

"I see. It seems that when you ran, you once again closed the door I opened. You will not see her again unless you are willing to." Deloris informs. Artemis shakes her head then stands up to go check on Raquel.

"O-ok," Diana exhales in relief.

"Tell you what. Let's get you something to eat," Deloris stands and helps Diana to her feet. "Find me a snack so I do not attack anyone in the office, then go report to Lawson. By then it should be noon. We can go to Albert's Place. It has a nice menu and does serve the snack I need."

A truant robot blows a whistle as it breaks up the small student audience and sends them to classes. Those that did not move fast enough are given fines and told to report to the school superintendent. A fate that none of them want to partake in. Raquel watches as Deloris and Diana walk back to the library, discussing the events that took place. The sophomore grumbles under her breath then turns and jumps when she sees Laurie standing within close range of her.

At the corner of the square, Diana pauses when she feels the hair on her neck stand up and turns in time to witness Laurie's apparent berating of Raquel. Deloris also turns to see what is distracting the intern and focuses on the blonde. A strange energy is surrounding Laurie seen even in the distance. The truant robot scolds the students for not adhering to the warning and gives them to the count of three to get started to their lessons. Laurie and Raquel leave the area to head to their separate class.

Diana and Deloris then continue their walk to the hovercar parked next to the library. The vehicle beeps to life and raises the door to allow the two officers to enter. Diana gets into the car and scoots all the way to the other side and as far away from Deloris as she could get. The senior officer simply sits in the car and allows the door to close. The vehicle then levitates off the ground, turns on its lights, and navigates its way to the exit of the campus.

An hour later, the vehicle arrives in front of the restaurant known as Albert's Place. The two officers exit the vehicle and Deloris sends it on its way, they will walk there once they are finished with lunch. This will give the senior officer time to evaluate the intern. The door opens to allow the two to enter the establishment. The holo-tube buzzes with media intrigue as a group of renowned senators proudly declare their sponsorship of the museum's exhibit of Amamet's tomb.

The sneak preview features small statues of a strange beast with the head of a crocodile, the front limbs and shoulders of a large cat, and the backend of a hippopotamus. A multitude of paintings and pictures depicting the same beast fill the many walls that they retrieved from the same location as the tomb. The owner of the restaurant mutters under his breath as he picks up a remote and turns down the media then returns to reading an old-fashioned newspaper.

The bell upon the door jingles, prompting the owner to look up from his daily read with a scowl. He glances at his watch, not expecting anyone to come in before the noonday rush. He straightens to his full six-foot height and runs his strong right hand through his frost blonde hair as he turns to greet his guests. Diana lets out a quiet sound of exasperation as she shakes her head when she notes the first destination of the restaurant owner's amber eyes fall upon her. She crosses her arms and watches as a feral grand etches onto his handsome features revealing two finely sharpened vampiric teeth.

"If I did not know any better, I'd say you are more wolf than vampire, Albert," Deloris speaks with humor in her words Albert tears his gaze from the young woman to her guide.

"Deloris, I apologize. I did not greet you correctly," Albert's feral grin dims slightly. "Welcome, both of you, to Albert's place. What can I get for you?"

"I need a warm snack to tide me over for a short while until I get home this evening," Deloris orders. She casually sits down at the bar.

"I'm not very hungry right now," Diana said, steadily meeting the restaurant owner's gaze. "I need a glass of water to rehydrate. Can I have it to go?"

"Of course, you can my beautiful, tender, morsel," Albert said seductively. He pauses when he hears Deloris clear her throat and note her very displeased look. "Ah, yes. Let me get those for you now." He leaves the two to get busy preparing their order.

The muffled excitement of the media barely escapes the speakers of the holo-tube as they spin tales and stories about the many exhibits located at the Museum of Past Modern History. A few of the anchors gleefully include controversial reports of some of the institution's most famous collectors. Diana shifts a little in discomfort as the media once again focuses on the newest exhibit, displaying the name and location. The display is quickly replaced by an animated form of Amamet devouring the hearts and bodies of people.

Diana looks up at the holo-tube as the beast turns its attention to the audience in the room and appears to jump right at them. The young lady draws a short breath and takes several steps back as her body starts to glow silver in color much too Deloris's surprise. The holo-tube suddenly explodes ending the transmission of the animated beast and the news coverage of the event. Diana falls to her knees as her breathing increases along with her heart rate. The lights flicker violently as her body starts to shake and perspire. Albert cusses from his kitchen as Deloris stands and kneels next to the intern.

"Fascinating," Deloris says, intrigued. "Diana relax, breathe, calm down. You are drawing on energies you do not understand."

"I can't," Diana says through grit teeth.

"Let me see if I can help," Deloris offers and carefully reaches her hand out.

"No! Get back," Diana snaps. Her voice seems to echo as if two spoke as one.

Deloris feels an energy push on her as if trying to get her away from the intern. Undaunted, she pushes back. A gasp escapes Deloris as she is picked up and toss away from Diana, knocking over tables and chairs. The force of which breaks at least three pieces of furniture in the process. Surprise soon gives way to anger as Deloris lets out a sound of rage and stands, her powers roaring to life around her further damaging more furnishings.

The senior officer carefully stalks back to the intern, barely maintaining the last threads of control she has left. The entire building shakes and moans as an influx of energies suddenly fills the space contained within. Diana claws at the floor as a surge of energy erupts from her and washes over the entire structure. As suddenly as it started, Diana's breathing begins to slow down as her pulse quiets to normal. Her shaking body calms down as she carefully flattens her hands against the floor.

Diana quietly mutters words of relief under her breath. The experience feels as if she has just finished running one of the hardest marathons in her entire life. Stunned by the sudden change, Deloris stops her advancement to keep her distance as she waits. The golden form of Artemis with her arm around Diana shimmies into full view as she stabilizes the intern.

The lights stop flickering, returning to normal operation as Albert walks out of the back kitchen. Diana struggles back to her feet, wobbling a little until she feels someone steady her enough to sit down. She places her arms upon the bar and then places her head upon her arms with a moan. Deloris cautiously approaches the intern and sits next to her still studying the young woman quietly.

Albert places two beverages in front of Deloris catching her attention. One is a shot glass full of a deep maroon liquid while the other is a large to-go cup with its contents hidden. He then places a plate with the grilled cheese sandwich in front of Diana along with a large glass of water. A to-go cup, also full of water, is set next to the original.

"What's this?" Deloris nearly growls. "I only ordered one."

"The shot is concentrated and, on the house," Albert explains. "I think you need it, so drink up before we have two testy vampires in the building." He turns to his second guest. "As far as you go, young lady. You have a grilled cheese in front of you. Eat it before you go since I'm sure you need to replenish your strength."

"I'm not going to argue," Diana relents. "What just happened to me?"

"That's what I want to know," Albert echoes and goes back into the kitchen.

"That makes the three of us," Deloris muses and studies the destroyed holo-tube as she finishes off her free drink.

The ebb and flow of traffic rushing by the tempered glass windows of the Middle District Police Department marks the coming and going of the noon hour. A modern building, it has many curves at odd angles covered in glass and steel. Three stories tall and as large as half a city block, it is divided into many units making up the law enforcement of the middle district.

Many of the units were formed through the years of political power plays to include the newest sector dubbed the Paranormal Investigation Unit shortened by the initials P.I.U. Currently, this new sector is a joke to the more established departments of law enforcement. However, in recent cases, the P.I.U. has risen above and beyond expectations and is starting to become essential to the policing community.

Located on the ground floor and off to the corner of a maze-like interior, the fledgling department has yet to expand beyond the founding members. The Commissioner, Lawson, has remedied that by hiring a few specialized employees and expects his new crew any day now. The doors to the P.I.U. sector open with a shush sound to allow two people to quietly enter.

Lawson gets up from his desk to peek out of his office and watches. Deloris pauses a couple of feet in front of the door. The commissioner frowns in concern when he notices Diana continues to walk into the space until she is sitting down at her desk. The clock on the wall strikes a quarter after noon briefly catching the attention of Deloris. Lawson decides to approach the senior officer as the clock quiets down. Deloris notes his approach and nods a greeting to the supervisor then turns her attention back to Diana. Lawson also focuses on the young woman and rubs his scraggly beard as he notes her sagging shoulders and refusal to make eye contact at the moment.

"You look worried," Lawson notes quietly.

"I am worried," Deloris admits. "Diana just went through two very different episodes of paranormal and arcane experiences. My concern is that one triggered the other and that she may not be done."

"Anything that requires a visit to the emergency room?" Lawson inquires.

"Still trying to determine that," Deloris said. "It involves her Aethoes."

"I see," Lawson rubs his chin a little, "I'm gonna talk to her."

The commissioner swaggers his way towards Diana with the senior officer quietly following. Even though he does not have any inkling of the paranormal or whatever an Aethoes is. He does have daughters and feels that his experience with them will assist him with this episode at least.

The sound of Lawson's footsteps barely reaches Diana's ears until he is only a few steps away. She jumps a little when a chair groans as he slides it into place and sits down, straddling it. Lawson focuses upon the intern as she turns to face him, especially her eyes. The commissioner's steely blue orbs seem to fill with understanding when he notices the different color that Diana's eyes have become. Behind him, Deloris quietly swears from the amount of energy coming from the gaze causing Lawson to simply smile.

"You're a beautiful young lady, Diana," Lawson complements. "But I didn't know that your eyes were that shade of green."

"What?" Diana blinks in surprise and her eyes go back to the normal blue-grey. "I'm sorry, a lot of things have happened today."

"I can imagine," Lawson sympathizes. "Want to talk about it?"

"Not really," Diana half shrugs. The sound of a spaghetti western theme song fills the room as Lawson removes his mobile device from his pocket.

"This is Lawson," he answers the incoming call, stands, and takes a few steps away, placing the other hand in his pocket.

Diana squints as a very high piercing ring echoes in her ears. A soft voice barely breaks through the ringing then is drowned out altogether. Deloris mutters in disbelief when she senses the rise in energy coming from the young woman. A golden flash briefly fills the room and blinds the senior officer temporarily.

Deloris clears her vision quickly then relaxes when she sees Artemis sitting next to Diana with her arm once again around the intern's shoulder. Diana focuses on the warmth she senses around her and gradually calms down as her body relaxes. Lawson returns to his seat and notices that it has moved closer to the intern yet appears empty. Rather than sit in the chair, he decides to simply stand next to Deloris as he places his hands behind his back and clears his throat.

Once he's gathered the attention of his employees he informs them that the girl from the frat house has passed away and that her parents request the case to be closed. According to the phone call, the girl has died of natural causes. There is a moment of silence between the trio as they contemplate the information for a moment.

"That does not seem right," Deloris said as she focuses on her supervisor. "What did you want to do, Lawson?"

"Procedures would dictate that we close the case and move on per request," Lawson quotes from the rulebook. He goes over to the window and looks out. "However, there is something going on. I need someone to go back to the campus to find a woman named Theresa. She's the one that contacted me about the First Night Party."

"I can go," Diana stands.

"Actually, I think you need to stay here and do a little online researching," Lawson suggests, glancing over his shoulder. "Deloris, can you handle this?"

"Sure," Deloris accepts. "Any obvious traits I need to know?"

"She sounded old," Lawson answers simply, "and very blunt."

"Right," Deloris rolls her eyes as she heads to the doors. "I will poll the teachers first. See you in a little while."

The doors close behind Deloris as she traverses into the hall. She carefully scans the area taking note of the various officers from different branches staring at her with a few quickly avoiding her altogether. One particular officer leaving the elevator quickly reverses and goes right back on the elevator to allow Deloris to pass. The door to the elevator closes and does not open as Deloris leaves the building.

Once outside, she uses her telekinetic abilities to order one of the hovercars to pick her up. The vehicle hums as it rounds the corner and comes to a silent stop so that it can open the doors that allow the passenger to enter. Deloris sits in the backseat and folds her legs as the door closes. The hovercar lifts up and does a U-turn to get onto the freeway and head towards Morstone University.

CHAPTER FOUR

Morestone's Hidden Secret

The ride to the university takes exactly one hour down the freeway from the police department. The hovercar's electric engine hums as it pulls to the curb of the main building on campus. Deloris stretches as the door to the car opens up to allow her to exit. Once she is out of the vehicle, the door closes. It hums back to life and goes to park itself in a designated spot. Deloris notices the sparsity of students roaming the schoolyard and finds it unusual. She approaches the entrance to the college and is allowed entrance as the doors gently slide open.

A couple of students hurry out of the building in order to get to their next class, fearful of the consequences if they are late.

Deloris enters the building after the small exodus taking great care to keep her identification badge on display to avoid confrontation with security. The cold stone of the hallway echoes as she traverses deeper into the structure. She peeks into various classrooms and sees that they are all empty. She enters at least one of the classrooms and notices that the teacher and students have recently left. Deloris furrows her brow inquisitively as she turns and exits the classroom to seek out the teacher's lounge.

A handful of students go through their locker before heading to their next classes located in other buildings, ignoring the officer. Deloris finds a directory that points her in the right direction and finally arrives at her destination. She finds that the door is locked tight and a little rusty.

Deloris mumbles a few words of curiosity as she takes a step back to focus on the lock. Seconds later there is a distinctive click as the door unlocks and she opens it silently. The empty room on the other side of the door takes Deloris by surprise as she enters the space. There are no signs of activity reflected in the thick layer of dust that covers everything and chokes the sunlight streaming in from the window. In the current condition, it is obvious that this room has not been used for a very long time.

Deloris runs her fingers through the dust and examines it carefully. The powder feels a little funny to her sensitive touch and she can't immediately explain why. Deloris leaves the room and heads down the hall. She runs into the student lounge much to her delight. However, is dismayed when she does not see a teacher wandering about. Instead, she sees a variety of students busy with their work and oblivious to anyone watching them. Deloris studies the scene for a short time then decides not to disturb the college students and instead seeks out the college superintendent.

Down the hall and to the right is another directory that Deloris uses to map a path towards the superintendent's office. Nearly forty-five minutes of following the university's substandard signage, Deloris manages to find the correct hall leading to her destination. The left side of the hall is a row of tinted windows to keep the pathway in a version of twilight. Upon the right wall of the space are many paintings and sculptures of the past college superintendents, each poised with either a blank expression or a scowl. There are many from times past that are human with a few representing visitors from around the known universe. All of them are male and sport a variety of facial hair of nearly all the styles from the past up to the present day.

Deloris lollygags down the hall as she takes in the rich history of Morstone University. She gets to the last painting and pauses to study it. The painting is a beautiful woman with the artist emphasizing her femininity. The woman's golden eyes and lush brown hair are perfectly depicted with a playful smile upon her lips. Deloris also takes note of the unusual jewelry that the current college superintendent is wearing in her picture. It is similar to the necklace that Diana found at the frat house.

"You have a lot going for you, Raine Pikeys," Deloris observes as she reads the plaque under the picture. "Let's see if you can answer a few of my questions."

The door to the superintendent's office is closed but not locked. Deloris easily opens it and walks right in. The waiting room of the office is decorated to look as if it came out of an old Victorian-era entranceway. The wallpaper resembles the same design from the fraternity house with loud flowers in various colors. A clawfoot chair, for decoration only, sits proudly in one corner of the office with an old-fashioned coat rack right next to it. The carpet is worn but still maintains its deep purple color. Lastly, the lighting is nearly too dim for any student to sit comfortably in the space.

The secretary robot activates and blips at Deloris as it scans her with a red light. The senior officer holds up her badge and announces her name to the mechanical being. The light on the robot turns green as another light blinks upon the wall nearest to Deloris. The panels on the wall quickly slide together to form a chair which the detective may sit on. The robot announces that it will inform Dr. Pikeys of the unexpected visitor.

Deloris sits down comfortably and places her hand upon her lap as she levitates her phone orb in front of her. The item lights up brightly as a holographic image of the school's webpage comes up. Deloris surfs until she finds the superintendent's profile and settles down to read it.

"I do not like them poking around," a male voice said with obvious displeasure from behind a second closed-door. "Are you certain they do not have the resources?"

"Of course, love," a woman answers. "The Paranormal Investigation Unit is a department created by the head senator as a political ploy. There is no real threat from them as they are simply pawns in this political game. From my understanding, they will be dismantled by early next year."

"And what about the girl?" the male asks.

"She will be taking care of in an appropriate manner," the woman assures. "What is this? It looks like I have a visitor."

The phone orb slowly lowers to Deloris's lap as it deactivates and her attention turns towards the voices beyond the second door. She turns to it as the door opens and Beryl exits the office ignoring the visitor as he continues his way. Deloris watches as the young man marches into the hall visibly upset from his conversation. She barely notices a cool shadow crossing over her. Deloris turns to meet the gaze of the superintendent.

"This is a surprise," the college superintendent said. "I did not expect the police to return. The girl passed away not too long ago."

"I've heard," Deloris agrees and stands. "Deloris Matox of the P.I.U., I am here to speak with you about a few of your students."

"Dr. Raine Pikeys," the college superintendent introduces. "Have a few of my advanced students summoned ghosts? This is the first I've had an investigation from the Paranormal Investigation Unit."

"Perhaps. Shall we go into your office?" Deloris asks politely. "Just in case someone walks in while we are talking."

"Of course," Raine smiles warmly.

The superintendent leads the way into her office carefully closing the door once her guest enters the space. Deloris glances around the room and sees the very large and imposing desk with no paperwork upon it. The carpet's purple color continues into this room as does the lighting. The wall behind the superintendent's desk is decorated with a multitude of degrees as well as two shadow boxes.

One shadowbox contains an unusual looking whip while the other holds a revealing leather outfit complete with a spiked collar. Dr. Pikeys invites her guest to sit down in one of two large chairs situated directly in front of the desk. Deloris decides to sit in the one closer to the door and sees that the superintendent is humored by the choice.

"Which student did you want to discuss?" Raine asks as she sits behind her desk.

"Let us start with the one that just left," Deloris offers. "Beryl."

"He is an honor student and has recently been voted leader of the Alpha Norma Sigma fraternity," Raine informs, her words are not very warm. "He has not caused any problems and has co-operated fully with police for their investigation. What did you want to know about him?"

"Let's start with how long he's been at this college," Deloris says calmly. "Has he been here long enough to graduate?"

"He has switched majors many times," Raine sits back and focuses upon her guest. "So, he's been here longer than most. As I said before, he is an honor student."

"Hmm...I see," Deloris focuses upon the woman's eyes. "How long have you been having an affair with him?" She watches as Raine's eyes widen before they narrow in anger.

"Get out," Raine snarls as her eye color changes to blood red. Her fangs protrude from her lips.

"Oh really? There's no need to get testy." Deloris shrugs not intimidated by the instant change. "He is quite a stud from what I see. I am just wondering is all? But, isn't it against school policy for college superintendents to have such relationships with their students?"

"I said out!" Raine repeats.

"I'm not done with my investigation yet," Deloris remains calm and places her hand upon her knee. "Now, shall we continue like civilized vampires or are we going to get physical or mystical? It does not really matter to me. I will have my answers one way or another.”

Deloris arches an eyebrow when she hears a deep growling sound emitting from the direction of the superintendent. The senior officer sits back calmly and is hardly surprised when Raine sends a strong wave of energy in her direction. The wave hits Deloris but does not affect her as she rolls her shoulders and glares at the superintendent.

Raine feels a stronger energy wave slam into her harshly, knocking her out of her chair and onto the floor. The superintendent snarls, briefly glancing at the whip as she stands back up. Deloris casually brushes off her jacket and once again meets the gaze of her hostess. She notices the superintendent’s nails dig into the wooden desk temporarily. As suddenly as it has risen, Pikeys’s energy level lowers and her posture changes.

“I see,” Raine sits back in her chair and focuses on the woman. “It is against school policy for me to discuss a student’s affairs to anyone but their parents. Especially since the case of the First Night Party has been closed by the police. Thus, Ms. Matox, you have no case or right to ask such questions. Now leave before I have you banned from campus for eternity.”

“Eternity is a very short time, Dr. Pikeys,” Deloris assures. “Very well, during the investigation, I noticed that there is a rogue vampire among the fraternity brothers. Do you care to talk about that instead?”

“There are no rogue vampires on this campus, Ms. Matox,” Raine informs. “The one that you saw in the frat house is possibly their guest. An alumni name Wyliam.”

"From what I have seen in my experience, he is definitely illegally changed. I am simply reporting it to you before I inform the correct authorities. Do you know who may have converted him?" Deloris asked. "Although, I may already know that answer."

"You are pushing a very thin line, bitch," Raine growls.

"No need to get offensive. I simply want answers," Deloris said calmly. However, she is slowly losing patience with the woman.

"You will get none here," Raine snaps.

"I see," Deloris stands up. "It appears that Beryl has a prized puppet in you."

The chair scrapes gently against the carpet as Deloris pushes it closer to the desk and turns and walks out of the room. She refuses to acknowledge Raine's glaring gaze as the door closes behind her. The secretary robot invites Deloris to take a survey which is politely declined. The senior officer then leaves the superintendent's area completely as she goes back into the main halls of the building. She finds a way to the entrance hall as a handful of students quickly sort through their lockers and head back into their appointed classrooms.

Deloris peeks into one of the classrooms and notices that the teacher is standing at the front of the class. Since the lessons have started, she decides to simply continue her slow stride until she reaches the exit. Deloris walks out of the building and grumbles; the sunbeams seem brighter than normal. With a slight clicking of her tongue, she pulls her shades out and puts them on to mitigate her sensitivity to the sunlight. Deloris makes a quick decision to go towards the frat house to see if she can gain entrance once again.

The unlocked door to the Alpha Norma Sigma fraternity house opens up with ease. Deloris enters the space and quickly closes the door behind her. So far no one is around and she assumes they are all in class right now. She takes off her sunglasses and scans the area noting that the underwear-ridden chandelier is now in the corner of the room. The wallpaper is also cleaned and looks to be brand-new. She looks up and sees a mural painted on the ceiling in place of the chandelier. There are a few Egyptian hieroglyphics intermingle with the rest of the fresco. The smell of fresh linen feels the air and heavy fans blow all around to dry the now clean carpets.

The space is void of furniture as the old fixtures are gone and have yet to be replaced. Deloris touches the wall. The decorative paper plastered upon it has a strange feeling to her fingertips, as if she is touching veins. The damask declaration upon the paper still reflects screaming faces within the loud flowery pattern. Deloris takes a step back and studies the pattern. She is barely able to distinguish that it did not quite line up in at least two areas. Upon examining those locations, she deduces that the person that hung the wallpaper did not pay much attention to the details. With a curious sound, Deloris decides to head upstairs to examine the room where the First Night Party victim was found.

Once at the top of the stairs Deloris finds that the hallway is bright and airy which is a stark contrast to when she first visited the house. She pauses as she feels that there is still something watching her. Looking up she sees a mural of naked women decorating the ceiling and that all their eyes seemed to be staring at the hall below. Strange symbols blend into the background of the women. Deloris compares the symbols from downstairs and those that graced the hall's ceiling. The ones she is studying among the nudes are ancient Greek symbols.

The ringing of a bell causes the senior officer to quicken slightly to avoid confrontation. The sound signifies that classes are changing with the possibility of a fraternity member showing up while she is in the house. She gets to the original crime scene and opens the door. The neat interior of the bedroom greets Deloris as she scans it twice and notes that there is nothing out of the ordinary. There isn't even a trace of dust left upon the wood of the floors and all the rose petals are gone. A brand-new bed replaces the one that the girl was found upon.

"They are very good house darlings," Deloris muses of the fraternity brothers.

She gets on her hands and knees to look under the bed and finds there is nothing, not even lint. Deloris stands back up as she folds her arms. Her eyes fall upon a brochure from the museum about the newest exhibit. She goes over and uses her telekinetic abilities to pick it up to get a better look at it.

Amamet's tomb has become a very popular exhibit and is very expensive to visit. There is a one-thousand- credit per person for the inaugural night that includes a beverage and hors d'oeuvres for consumption. Deloris theorizes that Beryl is either well-connected or well-to-do since he has at least forty tickets for the event in a neat stack next to his lamp. She places the document back exactly where she picked it up and starts for the door.

Deloris pauses when she hears and senses someone heading down the hall. She backs up a little and scowls as the steps come nearer. Deloris quickly hides behind the door as it opens up and a member of the fraternity glances in. He then quickly departs when he sees that Beryl is not there. The door closes and Deloris exhales as she figures it is time to go. She did not want to run into Beryl or any of his fraternity brothers.

Deloris opens the door, peaks out and sees that the searcher is down the hall. He walks into a different room as she waits for him to close the door. Deloris exits the room she occupies and heads back down to the first floor. She pauses in the middle of the stairs and listens. When she determines that there are no other brothers present, Deloris decides to head all the way down the stairs and out of the house.

Once outside, Deloris once again dawns her shades as she heads to a bench to sit down and contemplate the case. An elderly woman carrying an arm full of books shuffles towards the Expo building catching Deloris's attention. The senior officer stands up as the old woman disappears beyond the doors of the building. Deloris jogs a little to get to the building and enters it in an attempt to catch the fast-moving woman. She enters the hall and hesitates; the old woman has disappeared into the wide-open spaces of the Expo building.

The cafeteria is now closed and students only occupy the tables to do homework or personal business. Deloris crosses her arms across her chest and has a curious look about her features. She concludes that the old woman moves quite fast for her age. Deloris takes in the structure of the building as she slowly brightens her mood to curiosity. A hall occupies the wall where the frat house and the Expo building butt up against each other. She decides to head down the hall in search of the old woman, hoping to catch her.

The darkness of the hall heightens all of Deloris's senses as she carefully goes deeper into the corridor. After only a few moments she reaches the end of the hall and is greeted by a door to the classroom. The brass plate with the name Ms. Cummins is attached to the wooden door. Deloris tries the handle of the door and finds that it is locked which is no surprise. She takes a couple of steps back studying her surroundings, feeling that the shadows are hiding something on the doorframe. Deloris's senses alert her that she is being stalked. She quickly turns to see that no one is there. Deloris lets out a slight hiss and dissipates into a mist as the intruder approaches.

The mist lifts as the old woman tips closer to the door and pauses in apparent surprise. Ms. Cummins looks around to locate someone or something then grumbles as she shifts her book and digs out her keys. The elderly teacher unlocks the door and goes into the classroom slamming it shut and locking it behind her. Several moments pass before Deloris drops down from the ceiling landing quietly and studying the door once again. The lock clicks softly before the door itself creaks open a crack. Ms. Cummins marches over and yanks the door open only to see no one is there. The teacher swears bitterly as Deloris slowly fades into sight behind the teacher and next to a moderately sized desk. The senior officer leans against the desk as the teacher slams the door and gives a rude gesture to it.

"Perhaps you can help me, Ms. Cummins," Deloris requests.

"Mother's breath," Ms. Cummins whips around and holds her chest, falling to her knees.

"Apologies for the intrusion, however, you are no more frightened of my presence then I am of yours," Deloris remarks calmly as she sits on the desk.

"Fair enough," Ms. Cummins relents. "Can you at least help me stand?" She reaches out a hand.

Deloris scans the teacher as she crosses her legs. She sees and senses that the old woman does not need any assistance in standing. Something about her outstretched hand is very uninviting. Deloris met the teacher's gaze with a slight snort. The senior officer's eyes flash once as she uses her telekinetic abilities to lift the teacher rapidly.

Ms. Cummins gasps and shouts in surprise as she rises quickly to the ceiling. She stops a few feet from colliding with it and is then gently lowered until her feet touch the floor. Deloris smirks as she meets the now truly frightened teacher's gaze and sees that Cummins's demeanor has changed. The teacher calms her heart rate down as she scans her guest and nods in understanding.

"I see that you are not in the mood for shenanigans," Cummins remarks. "Can you at least introduce yourself before we chit chat?"

"That is reasonable. I am Deloris Matox, senior officer of the Paranormal Investigation Unit," Deloris answers calmly. "You are Ms. Cummins."

"Yes, I am," the old woman acknowledges. "I am the teacher for the subject Criminal Minds." She studies her guest. "P.I.U., eh? Do you know Diana Hunter?"

"A woman named Theresa contacted my supervisor about the First Night Party," Deloris ignores the old woman's bait. "He asked me to find her and interview her about the party and its now-deceased victim. Do you know where I can locate Theresa?"

"The girl died?" Ms. Cummins seems taken aback by the news. She covers her mouth and turns to face a blank wall, fighting back tears.

"Sorry for your loss. Was she a student or relative?" Deloris senses genuine sadness from her hostess.

"No," Ms. Cummins said softly. Her features suddenly turn to determination as she marches over to the wall and opens a secret chamber. "Come with me." She instructs and disappears into the wall.

Deloris stands and stretches momentarily as she debates her choices. After a moment, she follows the teacher into the hidden staircase. She hesitates when the wall behind her closes slowly bringing her into complete darkness. Deloris's eyes adjust immediately as she sees Ms. Cummins pop a light stick to illuminate their way. Deloris sneers at the light then follows the teacher as they descend into the depths of the hidden space.

The air grows heavy and still as if they have invaded an ancient tomb as voices whisper in the darkness. The two enter into a large area and Cummins places the stick into a holder in front of a mirror-like object. The item lights up and brightens the room slowly to allow time for the eyes to adjust. Deloris looks around the room admiring the many ancient treasures from various Egyptian dynasties filling the space. She turns and hesitates upon seeing the wall adjacent to the one they entered.

The wall has a large mural painted upon it that seems to have been taken straight out of an Egyptian Pharaoh's tomb. From left to right it tells the story of an abducted girl and her ill-fated destiny. It starts with a woman kneeling in front of a girl child and ultimately carrying her away. Next, the child is chained with arm splayed out as she is being tormented by two demon-looking creatures.

Beyond that are two men, one of which is kneeling, in front of a second adult female wearing a serpent crown. In the hands of the standing man is a black orb with beams flowing either in or out of it and several miniature people marching within the light. The next scene shows the priestess holding the orb and a beam of light flowing out of it and into the mouth of a beast. The little girl is now among the marching people, separated by her different colored clothing. Deloris once again looks at the mural from left to right and then focuses on the beast eating the miniature people. It is the combination of a crocodile, a lion, and a hippopotamus.

"The three 'maneaters' from ancient Egypt," Deloris recalls the history. "All combined to make the ultimate beast of nightmares. Amamet, Devourer of Souls."

"My sister drew these sixty years ago, a week later she was dead. The anniversary of which will be coming up in three days," Cummins said. "She died in similar fashion to the young lady you saw."

"Did she attend a party similar to the one that took the life of the recent victim?" Deloris asks.

"Yes, she did. Yet her role was not the same as the victim," Cummins says.

"I see," Deloris muses as she touches the mural. "I have seen this before, but where?"

"They have a replica of it at the museum, perhaps you saw it there," Cummins informs.

"No. I believe it was somewhere other than here in Middle District," Deloris assures. "Are you Theresa?"

"Theresa was my sister's first name. I tend to answer and go by it as I am too old to care what they call me," Cummins answers honestly.

"Do you have any more information that I can use for this investigation?" Deloris requests.

"All of your answers are in front of you," Cummins relays. "They are literally written on the wall."

With that, Ms. Cummins goes into the darkened stairway and pops another glow stick to light her way back to the top. Deloris hesitates as she turns back to the mural and studies it in more detail. When she is done, Deloris follows Ms. Cummins up the stairs leaving the glow stick to burn itself out. She reaches the top and finds that the teacher has departed her classroom.

Deloris leaves the room and ultimately the entire Expo building as she contemplates the teacher's information. The senior officer goes over to the bench and once again sits down upon it. Deloris takes out her phone orb and dials Lawson's number. It rings several times and then goes to voicemail. Deloris decides not to leave a message as she heads back towards her hovercar in order to return to the station.

A Poor Choice

Lawson's deep voice drones into the room from behind the fastened door of his office, drowning out the daily activities of the police department. Diana closes a folder that she is studying on the Alpha Norma Sigma fraternity and the now dismissed case of the First Night victim. She waves her hand over a light bar in order to turn on her computer and receives a beep of acknowledgment as the machine comes to life. A holographic screen projects at eye level and the keyboard comes into view upon the desk. Diana carefully logs into her accounts in order to continue her research online. She shivers a little when her senses inform her that someone is sitting next to her. Diana willfully ignores the presence as she focuses entirely on the holographic screen in front of her.

The internet browser comes up normally and whizzes to a search engine where Diana types in her query. It takes only a few milliseconds for the browser to return nearly half a million entries on the Alpha Norma Sigma fraternity. Diana decides to separate the information and only search for the history. She notices that the fraternity is only about one hundred years old, relatively young compared to other college fraternities. The internet also discloses that the original First Night Party was ten years after the creation of the Alpha Norma Sigma fraternity.

The first fraternity leader's name was Jock and he started the tradition of throwing women's underwear onto the chandelier in the hall. Other than this unruly behavior, there is very little information on Jock. During her scan of the history, Diana finds a link to an old newspaper article and clicks on it. To her amazement, it is about an apparent murder of a college freshman.

According to the article, the girl's name is Claudia von Burton. Diana recognizes that the last name is the same as Raquel's. She clicks on the link that is connected to the name in order to bring up a picture of the young woman. Just like Raquel, Claudia also has dark-toned skin. Claudia had sage green eyes that complement her dark brown hair that seemed to flow from the top of her head all the way down to her shoulders. She is wearing an Egyptian Ankh upon a golden chain around her neck.

Diana stands and quickly takes out the piece of jewelry that she recovered and compares the two. She is shocked to see that the necklace she holds in her hand and the one upon the picture of Claudia are one and the same. Continuing to read her history, Diana finds out that Claudia was a high school valedictorian and attended Morstone U. back in the year 3054. According to the police reports the young woman had gone missing after a party at the Beta Cosmos fraternity house which is the present-day Alpha Norma Sigma house. The mystery remains unsolved and Claudia is declared dead by her parents thirty years after she had gone missing.

"This solves the mystery of the necklace. Are you the ghost in the Alpha Norma Sigma house," Diana speaks quietly to the image on the screen, "if you are, then why did you aggressively charge?"

Diana sits back down in her chair as she continues to read the article. At the same time of Claudia's disappearance, there was a strange cult rising. At first, it appears that the cult was little more than a reemergence of Egyptian mythology. Then something hit the front page of a major newspaper. Members of the Beta Cosmos fraternity were arrested and charged with first-degree murder for performing human sacrifices.

The majority of their sacrifices are women and little girls taken against their will to an undisclosed location. The computer begins to hum as Diana clicks on another link. The hologram monitor suddenly disappears, surprising the intern. The screen is suddenly replaced by a holographic image of Amamet. The beast snaps at Diana and her Aethoes right before the machine and all the lights in the room go out.

Diana stands with a slack-jaw expression and is slightly panic by the events that just occurred. Next to her, Artemis is poise ready to defend against the now departed beast. The approach of an ominous presence draws both of their attention to the door as voices penetrate the silence. They barely notice Lawson coming out of his office and checking various workstations and concluding that all of them are dead. Diana listens and recognizes the two voices of the approaching visitors.

"Her student profile says she works for the P.I.U.," Raquel said to the one walking with her. "That vampire chick also works here. I just want to check on Diana and inform her boss of what happened on campus."

"So, she had a panic attack, big deal," Laurie scoffs. "What does P.I.U. stand for anyway? Pain in Uranus?"

"It means Paranormal Investigation Unit," Lawson corrects as the two enter the area. "What can we do for you ladies?"

"Sir, I came to check on my friend Diana and to report a complaint," Raquel said. "It is my belief that your senior officer has abused her powers."

"I've already spoken to the culprit about it and it will not happen again," Lawson says calmly. "To my understanding, it was only a training exercise, is that right Diana?"

"Yes sir," Diana acknowledges as she approaches her supervisor and stands next to him.

"I'm here to be nosy. I never heard of the P.I.U. before," Laurie admits. "What do you do?"

"As the name implies, paranormal investigation," Lawson reiterates as he turns to the intern. "Did your computer quit on you as well?"

"Yes, it blacked out as I was diving deeper into the information," Diana acknowledges. "From my understanding of what occurred earlier today, it may be some residue from my episode."

"Either that or the other tenants of this building are still having issues with us being housed here with them," Lawson gripes as he places a hand on his hip and stares out the window. "Tell you what, take the rest of the day off. There is no use in you sitting here idle. We will discuss the case tomorrow between your classes. As it is an open investigation you should not discuss it beforehand."

"Yes sir," Diana salutes the commissioner. Lawson nods and walks away confidently.

"I like him," Raquel grins. "Are you guys hiring?"

"That, I do not know," Diana answers carefully. "If you are interested, you'll have to talk to Commissioner Lawson."

"Interesting, maybe we could talk about the Paranormal Investigation Unit a little over lunch," Laurie offers. "I know a place in the museum that will not be crowded this time a day and my fiancé is waiting for us there."

"That's perfect," Raquel chimes. "While we are at it, we can talk about Morstone University since you just started this year."

"All the restaurants at the museum are uber-expensive not to mention that I just ate," Diana protests.

"Wyliam sent me a message requesting that we meet him there and he is paying for it," Laurie said smugly. "Apparently he wants to meet you."

"I don't want a meet him," Diana said.

Diana's comment falls on deaf ears as Laurie leads the way out of the P.I.U. office and is followed closely by Raquel. Diana grumbles a little then decides to trail after the two departing guests. She quietly listens as Laurie makes unfavorable comments about the new paranormal policies put into place by the Parliament of Peers. Diana senses that something is not quite right about the ex-cheerleader besides her egotistical and arrogant ways.

Raquel casually mentions that Laurie's fiancé is an alumnus of the Alpha Norma Sigma fraternity. Diana concludes to follow the two despite the expensive lunch so that she can gain more information about the fraternity. The trio gets to the doors of the Police Department building and pushes them open manually in order to exit the building. The power outage apparently affected more than just the P.I.U. office.

Once outside, Laurie hails a hover-cab and orders it to take the trio to the museum. Diana hesitates a little in getting into the cab when she feels a strong draw against sharing the vehicle with the duo. She shakes her head to clear it then ignores the warning and sits across from her hostesses. Artemis frowns as the door closes and the vehicle speeds away heading to the museum. After a moment she disappears in order to meet up with her mortal doppelgänger at the destination.

The Museum of Past Modern History sits exactly three miles from the Middle District Police Department in the trendy part of town. It is gigantic and takes up seven city blocks with plans to extend it to seven more as the intergalactic collection continues to grow. The hover-cab pulls up to the side of the building to allow a robotic concierge to open the door for the women. The trio exits the cab and is granted access to the museum via a side door.

Laurie admits with some arrogance that she has connections to get them into secret parts of the museum to include the newest exhibit that is opening tonight. Diana keeps quiet and simply listens to the woman brag. She has no desire to reveal her own connection to the museum and many of its exhibits, the bulk of which were discovered by her late father. She figures that if she starts it would be a very uncomfortable conversation with the braggart. After passing under the threshold and down a small narrow corridor, Diana notices that they entered the huge edifice via the art museum part of the building.

"Yep, we are going to Thalsberry Restaurant," Diana acknowledges mostly to herself.

"What?" Raquel turns to her hostess. "Laurie, are you out of your mind? The most expensive place here? Seriously?"

"Don't worry, I have credit there I want to use to celebrate. All announcements to be made at the table," Laurie assures. "We will be going past a few exhibits along the way."

"I'm familiar," Diana agrees. "I've come here often enough as a kid."

"And you're still a kid," Raquel teases.

The teasing words fall on deaf ears as Diana half listens to the conversation between Laurie and Raquel. The bride-to-be explains in her usual flare that the restaurant they are going to will not be as crowded as the outer restaurants and they are staffed by real people instead of robots. Diana barely hears the words as she takes in the sights of the vast collection from the intergalactic artists around the known universe. She stops in front of the statue of a crouching man with his hand extended to the observers and it looks as if he is offering to pull someone up.

The artists represented him in bronze down to the fine hair that tickled his chin. The plaque in front of the statue indicates that the subject is the legendary archaeologist Juke Hunter. The inscription goes on to read that he is responsible for the discovery of various major finds upon the planet Earth. At the end, it says that he disappeared in the wilds of the southern jungle never to be seen or heard from again. Diana looks up at her father's statue and touches his hand before she turns and continues down the hall easily catching up to Raquel. The college sophomore is standing in front of some statuary examining the plaques describing whom the edifices represented.

"Diana, do you have a twin brother?" Raquel inquires.

"Not that I am aware of," Diana answers carefully. "Why?" she pauses at the woman's side still focusing upon her with a curious look about her features.

"Just wondering. I know the statue behind us, you are a clone of," Raquel thumbs behind. Diana turns in the direction.

"Hmm..." Diana frowns a little as she recalls some recent memories.

"So who's this?" Raquel inquires and nods to the statue in front.

Diana turns and briefly sees the giant statue of a handsome man. Instantaneously, it turns into a giant ball of flames heading in her direction. Diana cusses and takes several steps back until she is up against the statue of Artemis. She sees the flames continuing toward her and shouts in surprise or fear as she shields her eyes, then closes them. When there is no impact, Diana slowly lowers her arms and opens her eyes to see Raquel looking at her in obvious concern.

Diana pushes off the statue she is leaning against still shaking from her ordeal. She finally steadies herself with the help of Raquel. Diana once again focuses on the statue of the man and is relieved when it does not transform. The depicted man has his nudity covered by a flowing toga around his waist and half upon his chest. He also has a large bow and is aiming it down the hall towards the Egyptian exhibit.

"Are you alright?" Raquel asks slowly.

"Yeah," Diana said, steadily. "The statue is Apollo. In a time long past ancient, he was worshiped as a sun god among other duties."

"Really?" Raquel turns back to the statue. "Was he like an evil sibling or something?"

"I don't know," Diana shakes her head and starts down the hall again. "Not so sure I want to find out."

Raquel studies the statue a little bit more then decides to follow after the P.I.U. intern as they make their way into the Egyptian exhibit. They hope to catch up with Laurie before heading to the restaurant. Neither notice the statues gleam a little before Artemis walks into the space next to the stone representation of herself. She watches as the two young women depart and see that they come to a fork in the hall. Raquel and Diana seem to discuss the possibilities before ultimately heading left.

A flash of light to her side catches Artemis's attention as she turns to see her brother, Apollo, leaning against the stonework representing him. A boyish, almost mischievous, grin plasters his face as he waves at his sister. Artemis rolls her eyes and walks after her charges. As she nears a sign she swears and runs after the young ladies noting that they are heading straight to the exhibit of Amamet. Apollo watches his sister run then leans back thoughtfully as he slowly disappears, becoming one with the lighting of the museum.

The halls of the Egyptian exhibits are bathed in simulated desert twilight and did not help Diana's overworked senses. Every once in a while, she jumps at the various shadows that reach for her from the ancient Egyptian carvings. A clowder of winged kittens mew as they study the statue of Baste, fascinated by the facts printed up on the podium. Both Diana and Raquel are careful as they walk around the group of fluff balls and continue searching for Laurie. A pack of large men studying the statue of Anubis only glances at the two as they walked past.

A growl upon the wind causes Diana to shutter and glance at the statue. To her surprise, it glares directly at her with angry red eyes. She shakes her head and focuses on the statue again noting that it no longer is watching her but is staring straight ahead as it has done so for centuries. Diana quietly reminds herself that she does not need an episode similar to the one in Albert's Place.

Eventually, the two young ladies round the corner and see the back of the woman they are searching for standing beyond the rope of an otherwise close exhibit. Diana freezes when she sees the name of the exhibit, Amamet, and takes a deep breath in. She feels a gentle yet firm pressure upon her shoulders encouraging her to exhale and stay in place.

"I'll wait back here," Diana volunteers.

"Ok. Let me get Laurie and then we can head to the restaurant. This place is giving me the creeps," Raquel admits and hurries forward.

"You are not the only one," Diana mumbles.

A group of colorful representatives of the Andromeda Galaxy wanders by as Diana waits as patiently as possible for Raquel to return. She watches as the sophomore approaches the senior class member and seems almost hesitant to cross the rope. Eventually, Raquel does cross under the barrier and reaches Laurie's side. She touches the bride-to-be on the arm and receives an angry glance.

Diana arches an eyebrow when she witnesses Raquel take a step back and barely hears a slew of apologies. Laurie then rolls her shoulders a little and turns to head back in the direction Raquel came from. When she moves, the statue of Amamet comes fully into view causing Diana to gasp a little as she feels something slam into her. The enormous statue is a full representation of the ancient beast down to the stringy hair also carved out of stone. It is the same beast that Diana had a nightmare about not too long ago.

The statue's head moves a little causing Diana's breath to quicken as she prepares for another round with the devourer of souls. A physical hand upon her shoulder causes Diana to jump a little and turn. Raquel carefully removes her hand and watches as Laurie chuckles from the freshman's reactions.

"You don't have to worry about that statue, Diana," Laurie laughs. "Unless you are from Ancient Egypt."

"This is the second time you've spaced out, I think you might need more food than you think," Raquel said.

"Something tells me that you don't have to be Egyptian to run into that monster," Diana corrects. "You might be right, Raquel, I'll see if I can find something on the menu when we get there."

Laurie takes the lead and heads down the straight hall following the sign to Thalsberry restaurant. Diana quietly observes the woman's humor disappear as they pass the statue of Baste. A number of the winged kittens quickly gets out of Laurie's path and hide behind the statue. Diana makes sure that the kittens are okay and moves on catching up to her two companions as they approach the statue of Pahkath.

Laurie nearly jumped out of her skin as they got nearer to the statue. Raquel comments that her two companions are both jumpy and perhaps hungry. Diana looks up at the statue of Pahkath and did not see any changes. Laurie simply indicates that she strongly dislikes felines in general. She explains that she did not expect the statue standing upon their path. Diana pauses long enough to read the plaque in front of the statue then continues her way, following her hostesses. It takes no time to reach their destination.

One of five eateries located within The Museum of Past Modern History, Thalsberry restaurant is also the most expensive. The restaurant boasts an eclectic menu of dishes from around the known universe prepared by a chef of intergalactic fame. This is the second time that Diana finds herself walking through the threshold of this eccentric restaurant. The first time she did so she was only a child yet she remembers the look of shock upon her father's face when the bill was brought to him.

Paraphernalia of the museum's most visited exhibits is displayed upon the walls and undoubtedly includes the newest exhibit within the Egyptian area. Diana glances at the poster and forces herself to ignore it as the hostess of the restaurant glides forward. The hostess is not from Earth but one of many known galaxies within the universe. Her light green skin and small body compared to her very large head are almost cartoonish in nature. The small hostess raises her tiny arm and levitates a few lunch menus above her head as she asks the three new guests to follow her. The trio obliges and heads to the corner of the restaurant to a very large booth.

The seating area is decorated with a picture of the Greek Parthenon adorning the wall. Diana sits down with her back to the wall and in front of the artwork. The menus are placed in front of the guests in the hostess floats away as Raquel and Laurie take their seats. Raquel picks up the menu and gawks at the price before she puts it down and takes a deep breath.

Laurie laughs at the initial reaction of her companion as she picks up the menu and reads through it thoughtfully. Diana flips to the end of the menu and decides to order the vegetable soup. Their server, a human, waltzes over and takes their order with a grin as he listens to the three ladies. He quickly goes to put the order in as a third member of the restaurant crew brings over a large bowl of appetizers.

"I have a question," Laurie says conversationally, "the investigation that your supervisor referred to, is that the one involving The First Night Party?"

"Unable to discuss an ongoing investigation," Diana informs.

"Last thing I heard is that she died," Raquel said as she picks up a roll. "The word is that life-support was too expensive for her family so they took her off and cremated her about an hour ago."

"Really. That is not only quick but highly suspicious," Diana sits back. "There has to be something else."

"We can just ask her. Can't you contact her spirit?" Laurie inquires. "That is what you do as a P.I.U. officer, right?"

"That is not as simple as it sounds," Diana answers bluntly. "First off, you have to know what you are doing. After that, it's years of practice to perfect that."

"Do they provide training at the P.I.U.?" Raquel inquires with great interest.

"Before you're hired at the P.I.U. you have to pass a test from the senior officer," Diana cautions. "I would recommend that you do not pretend to have a supernatural ability when you face her test."

"If that is the case, how did you become a member of the P.I.U.?" Laurie asks as she nibbles on the appetizers.

"It's quite simple," Diana said as she meets the woman's gaze. "I passed the test."

The server once again waltzes over to deliver the food for the three ladies. Accompanying him as a tall and ruggedly handsome young man with a crooked smile. Laurie makes a happy noise as she stands up and hugs the man planting a surprise kiss upon his lips. He stares at her momentarily. A sheepish grin plasters his face as she introduces him to her guest.

Diana scans the young man. Unlike the last year of high school that she saw him, he has been transformed into a vampire. Wyliam laughs a little and is gently elbowed by Laurie after she introduces him as her fiancé. Diana meets the man's gaze and frowns a little bit; he seems to be more nervous than what a fiancé should be. The news of which also surprises him.

"Well, you didn't grow much taller than freshman year, did you?" Wyliam addresses the seated woman. "You're still cute though, in an annoying kind away."

"Sometimes it takes more than a few years to change," Diana retorts. "Since when did you become a vampire?"

"Not long after high school, why," Wyliam boasts.

"Was it a legal transformation? Or were you at the wrong place at the wrong time?" Diana quizzes. "If my memory serves me right those in high school whose parents are vampires usually change during the sophomore year. You were human throughout high school and never transformed."

"Well, you see it's like this..." Wyliam stutters.

"He has no memory as to how he was transformed. It may have been an attack as he served in the military," Laurie explains in a huff. "It does not matter to me. I am a very happy woman from the results of his transformation."

"I hardly believe that you were in the military, Wyliam," Diana says.

"From what Laurie tells me it was a short stay," Raquel informs. "You didn't make it past boot camp, did you?"

"You got me there," Wyliam laughs a little. "Laurie dear, are you ready to go? We have to plan for our public party."

"What party," Diana inquires.

"Wyliam and I are hosting a public party at the Alpha Norma Sigma fraternity house prior to our wedding at the same location. The wedding is private, but I will invite you to the party," Laurie offers generously. "The location is a gift to Wyliam because he is an alumnus and former leader of the fraternity. Beryl is nice enough to let us use the house and it is the perfect location as I love the decorations."

"Besides the location and frat boy decorations, I do not think that it is a good idea to have a party at a scene that is now associated with the murder," Diana suggests.

"That's right," Raquel said excitedly, "that girl did pass away there. Perhaps you can hold a séance at the party, Diana."

"Not even on my best day," Diana refuses.

"If you happened to show up, Diana, I will likely know it because it will be storming outside," Laurie grins. "If you do appear, we will have nonalcoholic drinks for those of us who are still kids."

"That would include me," Wyliam volunteers. "I can't stand the taste of liquor."

"You say that now," Laurie scoffs as she turns towards the door. "I'm going to visit the new exhibit again then we will head out to the frat house. I will see you later, Raquel."

Diana stirs her soup as she ponders the scene she has just witnessed. It seems to be very clear that Wyliam is uncomfortable with Laurie declaring that he is her fiancé. The simple questions that she posed to him made him more nervous. Diana watches as Laurie goes to the counter and pays for the meals at the table she once occupied.

Wyliam, who was supposed to have paid for it, seems to stare at the woman for a long time and then follows her out of the restaurant. Diana turns her attention from the departed couple to the single lady that shares the booth with her now. Raquel busily munches on her sandwich and chips yet there seems to be a nervous energy about her.

Instead of engaging in conversation, Diana turns her attention back to her soup as she contemplates the opportunity presented to her. She knows that the frat house will be fully accessible to her during the party. She could easily slip away and walk around to investigate as the party escalates. A deep pressure surrounds Diana and she decides to ignore it. Instead, she finishes off her soup as Raquel finishes her sandwich and chips.

"It is nice of Laurie to pay for our meals," Raquel said conversationally. "Do you think we can catch up to them before they leave?"

"I do not want to go near that statue any more than I have to," Diana responds honestly. "Can you tell me more about this party?"

"You know Laurie. It's going to be big. It's going to be expensive. And it is going to be all night long," Raquel explains. "If you decide to come, plan to stay until it is time to go to class tomorrow morning."

"I see," Diana muses.

The sound of employees bussing dishes in the different conversations within the restaurant blend together as the two head out of the eatery and into the museum. The hustle of the visiting public is increasing as more people explore the wonders of the known universe. Diana quickly finds the short is way to exit the building, taking them past the Aligon exhibits in the process. Raquel, who has never been to this part of the museum, points out the familiarity of many of the statues between the two advanced races.

Diana purposefully ignores the taunting and inquiries of Raquel as she hones in on the exit. Once outside the two notices that there are no hover-cabs awaiting guests of the museum. Diana is undaunted and simply decides to walk the three and a half miles to get to her apartment. Raquel joins her in hopes to find a cab back to the college. She speculates that she should get some rest prior to tonight's event. During the leisure walk, the two speak a great deal about their high school days and in particular the ex-cheerleader, Laurie.

"Something has changed about her since high school," Diana speculates. "Every once in a while, I see or sense something dark emitting around her."

"I think that Laurie may harbor some abilities that we don't know about," Raquel hints. "I get the heebie-jeebies when she gives me her murderous stare after I interrupt her from doing something."

"I only wish the heebie-jeebies is the only thing that concerns me about her," Diana said matter-of-factly.

The sidewalks of the city are beautifully designed and integrated keeping those who walk them safe from the automated traffic hovering above the streets. Floating sidewalks provide safe passage when crossing the highway and into the residential district leading them closer to Diana's apartment. The path taken leads the two past the girls' school that happened to be in the shape of the Parthenon. Raquel recalls her mother threatening to send her to this unique girls' school since she would not behave as a child. Diana only gives a little smile when asked about her mother and any childhood threats. She did not answer nor did she give any details about her family's past. Two blocks later they stop in front of Diana's apartment building as the young woman finally comes to a decision.

"Raquel, I will be attending the pre-wedding party," Diana announces.

"Wait, what? Seriously? You're coming?" Raquel blinks as she stampers in her surprise. "Just like that?"

"Sure, why not," Diana shrugs. "What time does it start?"

"Ur um...eight. It starts at eight o clock tonight," Raquel stammers.

"Excellent. I'll be there around eight-thirty, give me time to get my homework done," Diana offers.

"Great! I'll see you there," Raquel nearly cheers. "I can't wait to let Laurie know, I'll take a picture of her expression and send it to you."

"I think I'd rather see it in person," Diana grins. "The hover taxi stop is just up the street. There are always at least three waiting to pick people up."

"Thank you and I will see you at the party," Raquel beams as she walks away in the direction indicated.

Diana waves to the young woman then turns to go into her apartment. The phone orb inside of her pocket rings and she takes it out. A picture of Deloris illuminates in the air indicating that the senior officer is calling her. She sees a number next to the pictures that tells her that Deloris has called a number of times throughout the day. After a moment's thought, Diana simply turns the device off and places it back into her pocket. She figures that she will call the senior officer back once she is at the fraternity house.

Diana shakes off a feeling of dread as she enters the threshold of the apartment building and the door closes behind her. Artemis watches after the young woman for a moment as she tries to figure out a way to get through to her mortal doppelgänger. She did not want to risk another episode of Diana's internal abilities blasting forth again since the first time nearly killed her. Artemis scowls a little as she searches for a clue to communicate with Diana. She glances over her shoulder and comes face to face with the Parthenon a few blocks away. An 'ah-ah' moment comes to Artemis as she quickly disappears.

CHAPTER SIX

Facing the Fear

The four-story apartment building stands ever proud as the last rays of the setting sun change the antique white paint into layers of orange and red. The long shadows of neighboring towers cascade over the elegant structure. Hovercars quietly hum as they shuttle passengers to a variety of evening destinations. Among them is a unique hoverbike powered by its rider. The bike comes to a stop just outside of the apartment building. The rider steps off of the bike and focuses upon the third story window on the left side of the building. Her mirror shades reflect the structure nicely as a few unforgiving words whisper from her lips.

Standing nearly six and a half feet tall she is and imposing woman some may say an Amazon. Her long strawberry blonde hair blows in the wind and bounces back across her shoulders as she takes in the neighborhood. She is currently wearing a tight white bodysuit that shows off the beautiful curves of her body. Just below the collar of the suit is a logo of her workplace, The Gersherin Price Laboratory. On the opposite side is the embroidery of her name, A. Melody Hunter, along with her job title of Director. She takes off her shades and glances behind her at the replica of the Parthenon before turning her light gray eyes back towards the apartment building.

"Alright, my little forest dweller," Melody said exhaling in exasperation. "Time for a talk." She walks towards the building.

The hologram tube continues to talk in the background as Diana concentrates on her homework. She turned it on in order to have noise in the otherwise silent apartment. The noise helps her focus upon the simple tasks that are due back to her instructors tomorrow. She taps a few keys upon her light keyboard as she wonders why she did not finish her homework earlier.

Diana looks up in the mirror upon her desk and quietly recalls the events of the day starting when Deloris came to retrieve her for what turned out to be a hell of a day. She turns towards the window silently recalling the events and hopes to put them behind her. Diana focuses her attention back to her studies. She is interrupted when the show upon the holo-tube that she currently ignores suddenly goes off and is replace by a news anchor.

The volume automatically increases as the sound of breaking news fills the room. Diana, slightly annoyed, turns to see the new exhibit at the museum with the exception of the largest piece now missing. Shocked and curious, she turns up the volume a little louder so that she can hear what the news anchors are saying.

"Yes, Trudy, it's true," the male reporter assures. "It seems the statue of Amamet has been stolen."

"That's interesting, Josh," the desk reporter observes. "How was it stolen? I remember that Amamet's statue is enormous."

"The police are here right now to determine that. As soon as I find out, I will let you and our viewers know," Josh answers.

Diana turns the volume of her holo-tube back down as she contemplates the report. There are plenty of art thieves, a number of them have mystical abilities. But who has an interest to steal the statue of Amamet? Perplexed, Diana turns her chair back to her computer in order to research her questions. She types in her browser and receives several links in response including the Beta Cosmos fraternity. A sound of intrigue escapes her as she reads through the contents upon her screen, unaware of her front door opening.

Melody quietly enters the apartment and uses her telekinetic abilities to quietly close the door behind her. There is a silent click as the lock upon the door turns in order to stop any further intrusion. Melody quietly takes in the condition of the small apartment. Her eyes rest upon the back of her little sister just beyond the living room at a desk. Melody shakes her head a little and then glances to her right to see Artemis standing quietly in front of a window staring out at the street. The Aethoes turns to face the intruders and is relieved when she saw who they are. Melody nods slightly in respect then turns towards her own Aethoes, it is time to get this little talk on. Athena nods and focuses her attention on the seated young woman. Diana rubs her neck and shoulders as she quickly glances at the clock.

"Oh crap!" Diana exclaims when she sees that it is eight o'clock. "I've got to get ready to go."

"Go where?" Melody asks. "I hope not to that party." She watches as her younger sister whips around. "Hello, Diana. I heard you had a rough day today."

"Melody," Diana scolds her sister as she her grits teeth. "Woman! You and Deloris. Please stop invading my apartment at will." She slams her fist on the desk in frustration.

"Then develop your abilities to stop such invasions," Melody counters and fold her arms. "I believe Deloris calls her an Aethoes. I think you need to reconnect. I assume you had a rush of bad memories when you met her today."

"Stop right there," Diana holds up her hand. "How do you know so much about my day? And how did you learn of the party?"

"Artemis informed Athena," Melody lifts one hand then the other in the directions of each Aethoes. "Athena, in turn, informed me." She places her hands upon her hips. "Are you still going to the party?"

"I am," Diana confirms. "I have to. It's the only way I know to solve this mystery. Something happened to that girl in that house. I want to find out what."

"I see. Tell you what, let's have a little talk about your day and the meeting you had with your Aethoes." Melody offers.

"I'd rather not," Diana states firmly.

"You mistook that as a request." Melody shakes her head. "I am leaving you no choice, sister. We are going to talk about this."

"And if I refuse?" Diana's features harden with anger. Melody simply arches an eyebrow.

The chair at the desk turns suddenly and rolls until it slams into the back of Diana's legs. The young woman cusses as she is forced to sit down. She tries to stand but feels a strong energy keeping her seated. Diana snarls, her eyes slowly changing colors as she glares at her sister. A crackle of energy surrounds her and starts to spread across the floor of the apartment, latching onto anything that uses electricity. Melody studies her younger sibling and then turns towards Artemis to see a golden glow about the deity.

With a nod of understanding, Melody refocuses on her little sister when she hears a sound of agitated frustration. Diana tries to stand once again and finds that she still cannot break free of her bonds. The energy in the room nearly explodes with the holotube going haywire by flipping to all the channels by itself. The stove and refrigerator open and close harshly as if invisible hands are playing with them. The computer receives so many commands it turns itself off rather than burnout its processor. Melody takes in all of the activity and then calmly walks over towards her little sister and pauses in front of Diana. She bends down to look directly into her eyes.

"Maybe if you calm down, you will be able to break my grip," Melody said as her light green eyes bore into those of her sister. "You pull from your Aethoes yet you do not want anything to do with her. Sorry, sister, but you are her doppelgänger whether or not you actually want to be."

"What…" Diana stutters as she blinks, her eyes turning back to normal. "Melody, your eyes are not as green. How did they change so suddenly?"

"I know that, they only turn when I am either pissed off or I'm drawing from my Aethoes," Melody said with a smile as she straightens up. "Then again, anger and strong emotions as such give a quick connection to your Aethoes. It is not always the best way to learn your strengths. But since I have your attention now, let me elaborate on how we got here."

Another chair from the living room pulls up behind Melody allowing her to sit down across from Diana. Athena and Artemis quietly watch as the older of the two mortals relays what she has learned to her sister. In a time long forgotten upon the mountain simply known as Olympus, there was a gathering of the Pantheon. They were sitting down for a feast when an unusual pain struck through all those who were present. It was quickly followed by a wave of energy that split the deities and half. These doppelgängers, the very first, were born out of the desire for vengeance by one person and her many allies. They were supposed to have killed the original deities during their most vulnerable state.

Another wave washed over them assisting the originals in recovery and through trial and error, they discover that the immortals and their mortal doppelgängers are linked. An attack happened fueled by the ancient enemies of the Olympians known as the Titans with both mortal and immortals battled and were victorious. As the mortal doubles grew older and reach the end of life, the immortals discovered that they could unlink from the mortal. However, they could not draw that aspect of themselves back into their being. It seems that the second wave, the one that saved them, also semi-cursed them.

"All right," Diana takes a deep breath and she finally digests the information provided. "How do I correctly reconnect to my Aethoes?"

"The connection is easy," Melody admits "however, I believe that before you connect to your Aethoes, you need to first face your fears. Tell me, what made you so fearful of Artemis? As I recall you were very happy to be associated with her up into you were around thirteen years old."

"I thought I was pretending," Diana said, "and that Artemis was my imaginary friend with a large bow and arrow. She was there for me when the rest of the family has grown or left. Especially when our mother was taken away."

"Yes, you had a strong bond so why did it break," Melody asked.

"It happened on the day that father and I went camping upon a dig site that he did not want to leave. The details are sketchy but I do remember a forest fire," Diana recalls

A high pitch ringing sound pierces Diana's hearing suddenly causing her to close her eyes and shake her head. When she opened her eyes, Diana sees a large fireball blooming towards her rapidly. She shrieks and balls up in the chair in order to protect herself from the approaching danger. Melody arches an eyebrow stands and turns to see what is attacking. She frowns when she sees only the front door and nothing else.

A powerful surge of energy brings her attention back to her younger sibling as she watches as Diana starts to convulse in pain. Artemis takes a step forward and falls to her knees, holding out her arm as she tries to reach her doppelgänger. Melody is alerted by the change of events and places her arm around her sister. She closes her eyes and concentrates on calming the impending explosion, doing so successfully. Diana's breathing slows back down to normal as Melody releases her sister and sits back down in front of her.

"What happened?" Melody asks.

"I saw a fireball coming towards me," Diana explains. "It's the same vision I've had at least twice already today. This will be the third time and the most intense."

"I see. Your road to recovery will take a very long time unless we can find you a powerful guide to assist you," Melody informs.

"Earlier today Deloris unlocked some memories I buried deeply in my conscious," Diana recalls.

"Ah, yes, she did only do half of the job before you fled according to Artemis," Melody said as she stands up. "Luckily is not hard to find her so that she can finish what she started."

"I do not think I want Deloris anywhere near me right now," Diana admits. "I've been ignoring her phone calls all day long and I know by doing so I've ticked her off."

"Oh, she will get over it," Melody assures as she turns towards the living room. "We can let her in now. Yes, I'm well aware of her temperament." She converses with her Aethoes. "No, we cannot send her to the underworld if she is uncooperative. Uncle Julius would enjoy that way too much."

Melody rolls her neck and shoulders as Athena crosses her arms, glancing at the door. After a moment, the deity simply walks away to stand next to the window. Artemis notches an arrow and pulls back on her bow, aiming directly at the door. As the divine shield goes down, the room turns red and the door to the apartment bursts open. Deloris enters the apartment in an obvious angry mood as her blood-orange colored eyes focus upon the intern.

Melody clears her throat before she steps between the vampire and her little sister. A golden light swirl around Melody then condenses in front of her to form a large spear. She holds it like a staff as she faces her opponent. Deloris focuses on Melody first then her sensitive hearing detects two other beings off to her left. She glances over to see a golden arrow aimed directly at her chest and knows that the second one would follow the first piercing her skull should she take another step forward.

"Hello Deloris. Count to ten and take a deep breath. It was not Diana that kept you out. It was me," Melody informs as Deloris slowly focuses on her. "We can go a few rounds if you like."

The eagerness of her sister's voice causes Diana to mumble a few choice words as she tries once again to stand. This time her legs do not obey her command. The entire room seems to escalate with energy as Deloris takes a deep breath and closes her eyes. The vampire then lifts her hands and lowers them as she exhales in the energy in the room returns to normal. Melody places the butt of the spear upon the floor and casually leans against it. Artemis quietly lowers her bow and un-notches her arrow to put both away.

"Attacking you in any way is a mistake, Dr. Hunter, which I will not make," Deloris assures. "Even in the worst possible mood I can get into."

"That's better, at least you're speaking now," Melody nods her approval as the spear disappears. "I got a little news that might improve your overall mood."

"I'm listening," Deloris says curiously.

"The news involves completing what you started earlier. It appears that my little sister wants to reconnect with her Aethoes," Melody said.

"Really, last time that happened she fled the museum before we could explore her connection further," Deloris explains.

"At that time, I was simply going along with you so that you could stop harping on the subject of my Aethoes," Diana admits. "Through family connections, Melody got wind of my plans tonight and explained to me the history of this unusual linkage. I think I'm a little more prepared now and once the door is open it should remain so."

"You're telling me that you want to go through the same meditative guidance that we performed earlier today and the results will be that you and Artemis will foster this link that you have," Deloris verifies.

"Yes," Diana said with confidence, "there is really no choice if I want to better control my own mystical abilities."

"Well said, Diana," Melody applauds. "Deloris, you did this before and I have a feeling that you've done it more than once in your lifetime. This time I think you should be a little more thorough with your guidance."

"Give me a minute," Deloris sits down on the arm of the couch and rubs her temples. "I have to take all of this abrupt change in attitude in."

"I say that you both get started before Diana changes her mind," Melody suggests and turns towards her sister. "And don't forget that you have to face the fear that placed a solid separation between you and Artemis."

"I didn't think that would be part of the plan," Diana states nervously.

"In order to keep you from hurting yourself and others, I suggest that you do this," Melody retorts.

"Alrighty then," says Deloris carefully getting to her feet. "I will need a snack before I attempt anything since the loss of my temper did not do me well. We will have to stop by Albert's Place so that he can give me a glass of the pure stuff. Then we will have to go to the Museum of Past Modern History in order to perform this exercise. There are several strong energies there that would make it a lot easier on us both."

"Sounds like a plan," Diana said. "I guess we should leave as soon as Melody lets me up."

"I loosened my grip on you a long time ago, sister," Melody informs gently and watches as Diana slowly gets to her feet. "You will be able to see and sense a lot of things when you reconnect. Take it slow and use those around you as your guides. If you need more guidance, I am always there to assist you."

"I know," Diana mumbles a little as she rubs her arms.

"This is a very big step, Diana. You should be nervous but not fearful," Deloris said as she places a hand upon the young woman's shoulder. "You are an extraordinary young woman and is about to become even more so. Let's go."

Diana allows herself to be led outside the door as she contemplates her situation. Artemis watches the departure and quietly follows after her mortal doppelgänger. Melody is last to leave the apartment and closes the door behind her. The robotic guard placed at the door of the apartment building moves around as it chants the words 'I am pretty,' waving its arms around franticly.

Deloris informs Melody that the robot was doing that when she arrived earlier.

The mechanical being whips around and charges at them only to be smacked harshly by Athena with her spear. The robot shuts down to allow the group to exit the building. Melody gives Diana a warm hug before she gets back on her bike and leaves the scene. With no more hover cabs in sight, Deloris and Diana decide to walk to their first destination, Albert's Place.

The night sky is brilliantly lit by the nearly full moon and is enhanced by the energy-efficient streetlights lining the path that is traveled. Deloris observes the quiet intern as they walk down the street to their destination. Diana's silence and the way she is carrying herself is very unlike the bold young woman from this morning. The elevated senses of Deloris honed in on the young woman's fear which feeds into her current predatory state of mind. She could hear the pumping of the blood through the major artery upon Diana's neck and knows where to strike in order to achieve maximum flow. Deloris takes a deep breath in and clears her throat to attempt to distract herself from her hunger.

"What is on your mind, Diana?" Deloris inquires in an attempt to make a conversation with the young woman.

"Facing my fears. It's not something I do every day," Diana mumbles. "When I think about it, it raises my anxiety level."

"I can tell," Deloris observes. "You don't have many fears that I have detected. I would dare say that what you are about to face is more a challenge than of fear. Once you meet it, you will be fine."

"I'm not looking forward to it," Diana grumbles, "but I'm not going to back down either."

"That is what I want to hear," Deloris grins as they pause outside of Albert's Place. "Wait right here and I will be right out. Can I get you anything?"

"I am fine, thank you," Diana assures and watches the senior officer walk into the establishment.

The three-mile trek to the museum seems shorter at night compared to the day. The illusion of the moonlight in the empty streets aided the dual with their brisk travel. Diana feels a strange sensation when they break from the shadows of the buildings and into direct moonlight. She is not entirely sure if she likes the sensation or if it is slightly annoying.

The two arrive at the west side of the Museum of Past Modern History and are greeted by the chiming of the hour. The outside façade hosts a variety of languages to include the decorative ancient hieroglyphics of Egypt and the Maya. Ancient Egyptian and modern statues form pillars to hold a portion of the roof up and creates a small alcove to protect visitors from the weather.

Gargoyles hold sentry on the top of the building and grimace at those who pass by. The two unexpected night visitors continue to study the decorations as they walk closer to the building. Diana suddenly pauses and gawks at the statues. Deloris, seeing this reaction, simply pauses and continues to slurp on her to-go cup as she watches the intern.

Diana witnesses the crocodile statue suddenly snap its jaws and twist the head free from the building. She drops several unkind words and stumbled backward losing her footing as she falls onto her backside when the statue reaches for her. The statue of Horus, next to the crocodile, grabs the living statue and pulls him back in place. The crocodile statue growls in protest as it settles back down. Diana slowly returns to her feet as Deloris draws a long draft upon her drink. The statues are now back to normal with no visible signs of damage or detachment.

"What did you see, Diana?" Deloris finally inquires.

"Crocodile came to life and the hawk dude pulled him back in place," Diana explains in short. "Am I losing my mind?"

"The answer to your question is no, you are not. However, I did not see the attack," Deloris sips again as she ponders. "You should start working on your supernatural defense skills in a few days to let your awakened abilities settle a little."

"I have a feeling that I might need that training beforehand," Diana said as she stares at the statues.

The door on the opposite side of Horus opens to allow a small being to depart the museum. He is a feline and is known on this planet as a Seraph Cat. Like so many extraterrestrials he is from one of the galaxies of the known universe whose home planet was destroyed long ago. Yellow-green humanlike eyes scan the area around him as he sits down and gently touches his collar in order to summon his limousine. He is the size of a domestic cat typically found on this planet, Earth, with the coloring of a tan tabby with brown and black stripes. His small wings wave a little bit as he stands and stretches in order to work out a few kinks in his back. His tail lifts high into the air and has a slight curl to it as he awaits his ride.

Deloris grins when she sees the feline knowing that he is the curator of the entire museum system of the Milky Way. The senior officer decides to approach the thought ridden creature carefully as she does not want him to bolt. Diana cautiously follows and gives the statues a wide berth in the process.

"Nako," Deloris says in a normal tone and causes the cat to jump and bristle in fear as he arches his back. "Sorry about that. How are you doing this evening?"

"One life less," Nako said, his voice sounding like a child, as he relaxes and sits down. "Why are you scaring the wits out of me, Deloris? And who is your pretty friend?"

"Tsk curator Nako, you mean you do not recognize her," Deloris scolds mildly as she takes a sip from her cup. "Diana, can you step into the light and give the old cat a good look at you?"

"Good evening, Sir," Diana greets carefully as she walks into the lights of the museum. "It's been a while since I've come here to visit you. The last time I saw you, I was traveling with my father, Juke."

"Juke...Hunter," Nako tilts his head from one side to the other as he figures out the puzzle. "Oh! Oh! You are the little one, Diana. Wow, you've grown into quite a beauty."

"Thank you, curator," Diana acknowledges. "You're still fuzzy."

"I pride myself on my fuzziness," Nako boasts a little and then pauses as he stares past the young lady. "Wait, there is something or someone standing next to you. Are you summoning or haunted by ghosts?"

"Not exactly," Deloris informs and draws on her beverage again. "Don't worry, she'll come into full focus once we are done which leads me to why we are here. Can I borrow the museum again for about an hour?"

"You do realize that there is an ongoing investigation about our missing statue," Nako informs. "I do not want to risk you holding a séance or something like that while we are trying to solve this case."

"What statue is missing?" Deloris asks.

"The statue of Amamet," Nako answers. "It is a very strange case and perhaps it is good that you and little Diana are here. I know at least you, Deloris, are part of the newly formed Paranormal Investigation Unit."

"This is true; however, I have a priority to assist Diana with contacting and connecting with her Aethoes," Deloris informs. "We can investigate the statues disappearance after I complete my current task."

"If it helps curator Nako, once we are done perhaps Artemis and I can figure out what happened with the statue," Diana offers.

"The statue," Nako sits down and ponders as he contemplates the words of his guests. "How can the statue of Artemis help us in recovering the statue of Amamet?"

"We can find that out once my task is done," Deloris offers

A few lofty clouds briefly cover the moon as Nako stares at Deloris in contemplation. Diana rubs her arm a little to warm up from the sudden chilly breeze that surrounds her. The senior officer simply continues to drink from her large to-go cup as she meets the curator's gaze. Nako looks from one woman to the other with his small wings moving back and forth in time to his swishing tail. Deloris finishes off her drink and smiles at the Seraph Cat reassuringly. Nako finally lets out a soft mew in defeat.

"All right Deloris, you have my curiosity," Nako admits. "In order to keep my guard robots from bothering or disturbing you, I will accompany you."

"That's fine with me," Deloris accepts as she causes her empty container to erupt into flames. "Let us get started, shall we?" Deloris walks into the building unchallenged and is followed closely by Diana.

"Living statues? What matter of madness is that vampire up to?" Nako muses as he stands and shuffles after the women.

The floor of the museum echoes with the footsteps of the two guests. Nako prances into the lead with his tail held high as he shows the way towards the Ancient Greek exhibit. Deloris quietly chuckles at the cat deducing it is true feline fashion to lead the way. Diana absentmindedly walks next to Nako in silence as they approach their destination.

Different from this morning, Diana finds herself walking past other statues in the exhibit instead of shortcutting from the side. The first statue they come across in the Greek and Roman exhibit is that of Aphrodite with her arms raised in greeting. They shuttled past a statue of Zeus seated upon his throne with his hand on his hip and the other leaning upon his lap as he seems to stare at those that would examine him. Diana figured that the statue, similar to her father, was getting ready to lecture someone.

Guard robots prowl the structure and allowed the intruders to continue their way once they sense Nako is among them. The trio round a final corner and pause when they see a mirror with a bow carve into the glass. Diana focuses on her image and notices that the bow is in line with her left hand. She takes a step back from the mirror and continues to follow Nako as they approach the giant statue of Artemis.

"Here we are," Nako announces. "So, tell me, Deloris, how will the statue come to life?" "

"I never claimed that I would bring the statue to life only that I have a task to assist Diana to reconnect with her Aethoes," Deloris reiterates. "In this case, her Aethoes happened to be Artemis."

Diana approaches the statue and takes a deep breath in and slowly let it out as she looks up at the familiar features of the edifice. She places her hands upon her hips and tilts her head all the way back to look up at the ceiling. A painting of the night sky greets her along with the phases of the moon and an ancient text. She makes out a few words that mention Artemis's parentage and a few of her deeds leading to the present day.

Diana brings her head back down and looks across the hall to the statue of Apollo. The flashback of a fireball in the sky slams into Diana causing her to stumble backward and shake her head to clear it. She turns away from Apollo's statue and faces her companions.

"Okay Deloris, whenever you are ready," Diana surrenders.

"The question is are you ready? Once we start there is no changing your mind," Deloris offers one final moment for the intern to confirm her decision.

"I know that but like you mentioned this morning I have to face it sooner or later," Diana said. "I decided now is as good a time as any since I have a feeling that Melody would not let me up until I agreed with her anyway."

"Yes, your sister is very persuasive," Deloris agrees.

"This does not involve bloodshed, does it?" Nako inquires.

"I sure hope not," Diana said.

"For all of our sakes I hope not," Deloris resounds. "The snack that I got at Albert's Place should negate any kind of bloodshed that may have occurred otherwise." She sits down on the back of the statue resembling a running hound. "This time, Diana, I am going to go in very deeply to your subconscious so you will be placed asleep. This is done just in case I encounter something that brings on pain."

"Then I think it is best that I lie down instead of sitting down so that my head does not strike the marble floor," Diana muses as she sits down under the statue in finally reclines next to the giant foot of the edifice.

"Oh indeed," Deloris grins. "Close your eyes and relax your mind. Allow me to help you eliminate the chains that you have placed on yourself. Let it go..." she says hypnotically.

The lights around the museum turned off one by one leaving only ambient lights in the ceiling of the exhibit the only source of illumination. Nako watches and listens as he settles down upon his belly directly in front of Deloris. He starts to purr and his tail moved gently as he senses that something good is about to happen. Nako tucks his wings close to his body as the light around them starts to darken slightly.

Deloris stands up and walks over towards Diana as she continues to speak hypnotically. She sits down upon the large foot of the statue in tucks her legs under her as she concentrates upon the young woman. Diana is now fully asleep. Deloris positions her palms up and touches her middle finger and thumbs together as she then closes her eyes.

Deloris focuses on her breathing and soon finds herself literally flying into Diana's mind. She remains calm as the scenes continue to change rapidly around her. At one point the pace slows down enough for Deloris to see Diana as a small child runs into the arms of Artemis for a hug or protection. The pace increases again flying past much of the young woman's childhood.

Deloris folds her arms when the scenery once again increases in speed and she guides herself to the source of Diana's fear. Instead of a fiery hell, Deloris finds herself standing in the middle of a deep green forest. The woodlands are a mixture of evergreens and deciduous trees with several piles of underbrush mounted to the sides of a carved-out path. The sounds of the woodland residence are so vivid that it feels as if she is actually transported to a real forest.

"Hello Deloris," Diana greets and ducks the reaction from the senior officer.

"Never sneak up on me like that whether it's real or in a situation such as this," Deloris warns. "You are stronger than you thought considering that you found me. That is not an easy task."

"I'll keep that warning very close since I like my head upon my shoulders," Diana acknowledges. "Safe to say that we are in my mind."

"Yes, most specifically at the heart of your fears," Deloris explains. "Where is this place?"

"This is the forest where I went camping with my father," Diana explains.

"Ah, I see. Shall we get started?" Deloris requests as she takes a step forward.

The sounds of monkey calls reverberate in the trees above and around with a few of the animals crossing the path oblivious of the presence of the intruders. Deloris explains to Diana that they are watching her memories and are not actually in the location. Diana nods in understanding until an acorn falls and hits her shoulder. She looks down at the item and then backs up at the senior officer noticing that Deloris did not see the transaction.

The door to an otherwise hidden hut opens up causing the animals to scatter away. A tall and strong man exits the structure much too Deloris's delight. She scans the figure appreciatively. His white hair is cut short just above his neckline and mixes with his beard and mustache. He stretches, reaching for the sky until something distracts him and he turns his electric blue eyes towards the path that the two witnesses are standing on. Deloris and Diana move out of the line of sight to stand slightly off-center to view the entire scene. The man crosses his arms and grumbles as the sound of thunder rumbles in the distance.

"I am not in the mood for this today," the man, Juke Hunter, grumbles with the voice as deep as the thunder. "Diana, come here."

"In a moment, Papa. I'm trying to figure out what type of snake this is," a child says from the direction of the witnesses.

Diana shakes her head as Deloris turns to see that a child version of the young woman is actually playing with a large black hooded snake. The girl is around thirteen years of age and seems as fearless as the adult version. The snake tries to slither away but fails as the girl gently captures it by the back of the head and lifts it off the ground. Juke makes an exasperated sound as he holds his head and shakes it. This is his youngest child and he swears that she will put him in the grave before she reaches maturity.

"It's venomous, Diana, please put it down," Juke requests. "Come here, there are strangers coming up the path."

"There are," Diana the child responds as she walks out of the adult version. "Do you want me to go get the police?" She drops the snake and allows at the slither away.

"No, the police will not be able to deter these hoodlums," Juke says and then turns as several dark figures walk into the scene. "Who are you, strangers?"

"We know who you are in you have a connection to Zeus," the strangers counter.

The voices of the strangers cause Diana, the adult witness, to mutter under her breath as a burning sensation envelope her body. The strangers sound mechanical yet they are human in appearance. Deloris focuses on the strangers as if to determine where in the known universe they could be from. The strange beings lumbered into the light causing Juke's features to change ever so slightly.

"Run Diana," Juke orders gently, "as fast as you can and do not look back." He turns to face the strangers.

"But," both the child and the adult Diana said at the same time, "where do I go?"

"The forest," Juke answers as storm clouds begin to gather. "Your friend is there and will protect you. Always trust her, okay?"

"I," the child starts.

"The girl is linked with Artemis, kill her," one of the strangers orders. The voice is different from the original spokesperson. It sounds more human and feminine.

The child jumps back and dodges the first stranger the tries to tackle her. She goes around a second and through the legs of a third as she takes off running into the deep woods. She hears her father's voice as her pace continues to rapidly increase. Deloris and Diana walk alongside the fleeing preteen. The crashing thunder, as well as falling trees, cause fear to swell in the child as her pace once again increases. The adult Diana notices a glow about the child version of herself as the speed of running soon becomes unnaturally fast. Unlike the child, the adult knows that she is running full speed to nowhere.

Lightning crashes down into the forest and ignites the dried leaves and bushes immediately. Those strangers that are pursuing the child cry out in pain or anger as they lose sight of their prey. The younger version of Diana slows down and stops to catch her breath. The whoosh of the flame is preceded by fire itself as it surrounds the girl on three sides. Young Diana cries out in fear as her eyes widen when she sees the flames around her. The girl turns and starts to run down the only path that is not full of fire. A bright flash of light fills the clearing behind the fleeing girl briefly.

"Diana!" Artemis shouts then cusses as she quickly takes flight after the fleeing child.

"Interesting," Deloris muses as she once again walks alongside the running pair.

"This is where things start to break apart," Diana assures as she keeps up with the senior officer. "Right after the cliff."

"I've a feeling that we are watching both yours and your Aethoes' memories and they are being stitched together," Deloris remarks.

The young Diana sees the cliff in time to swear and slide until she stops just shy of toppling over the edge. Both versions of Diana, the girl and the adult, turn to the forest to see that it is now completely on fire. She has nowhere to go and a wall of flame is spreading toward her rapidly. The girl backs up and slips, nearly falling off the cliff. Artemis appears in time to grab the girl by the shirt and lift her up. The young Diana grabs the arm that is holding her, fear in her eyes as she wonders what is going to happen next.

The sky lights up as if it too is on fire as a large ball of flame careens at the two on the cliff. Artemis looks up briefly before turning to her younger doppelgänger and telling her to close her eyes. The girl instead looks up to see the fireball and cries out in surprise. The flames of the woodland reach forward as Artemis turns and tosses the girl off of the cliff.

The fireball screams past and nearly drowns out the cries of younger Diana. Artemis jumps when it passes the cliff in the forest fire claims the last space that she occupied. The two invisible witnesses are now flying next to what was the fireball and witnesses that the girl is now unconscious and caught in the arms of a masculine chariot driver. Apollo glances over his shoulder when he hears his twin sister land behind him. He then focuses upon the girl he caught in his arm, nods, and uses the reins in his other hand to guide his galloping steeds back up.

The horses snort as they obey his commands and pulled up rapidly, turning back towards the cliff. Artemis pulls her bow and takes aim at the forest fire as it forms into a strange creature. The flame beast growls at the group as they come within range of it. The river below the cliff is winding peacefully, oblivious to what is happening above. Instead of aiming for the flames Artemis decides to focus on the base of the cliff. Her arrow lights up briefly before she releases it.

The bolt screams as it sails to its destination, striking the cliff and causing it to explode. The beast of flames shrieks as it falls into the river below. Lightning careens across the sky, ripping open the clouds to allow a hard rain to fall. The deluge rapidly douses the fire as it cries out then dies. Deloris takes in the entire episode that she just witnessed with a nod of appreciation for the young intern and her Aethoes.

"It appears you had quite an adventure, Diana," Deloris notes and turns to her silent companion. "Are you alright?"

"I don't know," Diana says softly. "She saved my life."

"She saved the life of you both. Remember you are linked to her. If she did not save you, she too would have perished," Deloris explains gently.

The scene changes suddenly to where the horses are now landing upon the ground. Their hooves pounding any rocks under them to powder. The horses' orange glow fades as the chariot driver and his sister disembarks. Apollo appears humored while Artemis rolls her eyes at whatever bantering she endured. Juke hurries over to them with a worried look upon his features when he notices his unconscious child. He accepts the girl from her saviors and listens as they provide a few words of wisdom.

Juke makes a sound of relief when he hears the girl groan in her sleep and feels that she will be fine. He nods respectfully and turns to walk away as Apollo returns to his chariot and boards it. With a flick of his wrist in a crack of his whip, he commands his stallions to go. The horses pick up speed quickly as they gallop down the path and then jump into the air. Diana, the adult, feels the heat of the beasts and feels a few dust particles strike her as they careened past them. This time Deloris feels the same thing and frowns wondering just how invisible they actually are. The scene around the witnesses starts to fade as Artemis waves to her departing twin brother.

"Something does not feel right here," Diana expresses her thoughts.

"You are right, there is a surreal air about this area," Deloris agrees.

Flames erupt around Diana and Deloris suddenly and fill the entire void with fire. Diana shrinks back from the fire at first then shakes her head and takes a couple of steps forward. The flames represent her fears and now that she knows the truth about the ball of fire that careened towards her as a child, she feels that she is strong enough to face them. A feminine voice speaks in an ancient language as it commands the flames to attack. Diana recognizes the voice as the same one that accompanied the strangers that day in the forest. The energy level in the space builds up to a very high level as Diana sneers at the fire.

"I am not afraid of you, not anymore," Diana announces to the flames.

The flames roar as they twist into a column and attack the young woman. Diana holds up her hands and appears to catch the head of the column and hold onto it. The fire increases its pressure, pushing the young woman back until she is only inches from Deloris. The senior officer watches as Diana's body starts to glow silver and it spreads to the column flames. Half of the column suddenly disappears into nothing but smoke as Diana straightens up and a bow appears in her hand. The young woman pulls back and releases her arrow into the base of the fire column as a golden arrow flies past and strikes the top of the same creature.

Deloris turns to see Artemis floating a short distance away and focused upon the battle at hand. Diana reloads at the same time that Artemis does in both release their individual arrows at the heart of the column. The dual arrows penetrate the flames and cause them to explode outwards and dissipate. At the same time, the invisible owner of the voice screams in violent frustration and the void dissipates back into woodland. Diana lowers her weapon and takes a few shaky breaths in and out. The bow and arrow disappear as she falls to her hands and knees, exhaling once more in relief.

"That was very interesting, Diana," Deloris says of what she witnessed. "Not only have you learned of what happened that day but you also learned that your Aethoes is also your protector."

"The flames were a combination of an enemy and a rescuer," Diana recollects. "It all happened so fast that I blurred the two together."

"I think you did an adequate job of facing your fear and finding the truth that fostered them," Deloris offers. "After your father took you away, what happened?"

"I woke up," Diana admits.

"At this junction, I think that's a good idea," Deloris nods as she lifts her hand and snaps her fingers.

The light in the museum begins to brighten once again as the other areas turned back on. Nako, half-asleep, opens his eyes and stretches with a mighty yawn. The curator casually glances around to see Deloris stretching as she wakes up from her meditation and notices they now have one more person in the room with them. Nako sits down and rubs his eyes as he stares with an open mouth at the new lady in the room. Artemis focuses on the curator and smiles as a silent greeting before she turns her attention towards the sleeping young woman.

Deloris stands and walks away to sit once again on the back of the hound statue. Diana groans and moans as she stretches and then exhales a sigh. She grumbles about the light in the room and the timeframe in which she is awakened. After a while, she opens her eyes and sees a fuzzy image of the ceiling at first. Diana blinks a little and stretches again as she turns to one side.

Artemis smiles a greeting at her mortal doppelgänger as the young woman blinks and sits up slowly. Diana carefully gets to her feet as she quietly reminds herself to remain calm and breathe through the second encounter of the day. She rubs her arm a little as if to warm up or brush some of her nervousness away as she focuses upon her Aethoes.

"All this time I thought you were trying to kill me when you tossed me from the cliff but in reality, you saved my life," Diana carefully addresses her Aethoes. "I'm sorry, Artemis, that I thought you were something other than a friend after that encounter. I did not understand what happened at that time but now I do." She blinks back tears as Artemis places a hand upon her shoulder.

"Wow, there are two of them," Nako said in awe. "Deloris, how is this possible?"

"Shh," Deloris scolds gently. Nako's features change to that of confusion.

"The fire, the cliff, and the strangers. What were they? And who was the voice commanding the fire monster?" Diana inquires then appears confused at the answer. "Really, Medea?"

"I seriously hope not," Deloris muses and is shushed by Nako. She glances down at the cat to see him smiling, cheekily.

"Yeah, we will get to that after we solve this Amamet mystery," Diana agrees with Artemis. "How do I do this reconnection that Melody was talking about?"

The illumination of the room softens as Artemis simply lifts her left hand and focuses her attention on Diana. The young woman has a slightly worried expression at first and then takes a deep breath in and straightens her posture. Diana's features turned to determination as she lifts her own hand, facing her Aethoes.

Slowly, the two move towards each other as a bright green glow surrounds them. As the two grasp hands, the glow brightens enough to blind the witnesses in the room. Deloris hisses and growls as she covers her eyes from the unexpected intensity of the light. Nako sneezes violently from the brightness until the light dies back down to a normal level. Diana is standing with her eyes closed at first then opens one eye then the other when she notices that only her hand is still lifted into the air. She brings it back and studies it is seeking any identification marks upon her skin.

"That felt a little weird. Not sure how to describe it," Diana admits in looks up when Artemis simply nods to her. "All right, I can hear you a lot clearer in my mind and I see you a whole lot clearer. I think I'm going to need to understand what has happened."

"As your sister alluded to, take your time," Deloris offers.

"So, you are telling me that Diana Hunter and the Greek goddess of the hunt, Artemis are somehow one entity? Or that you somehow brought Artemis to life, Deloris?" Nako inquires as he tries to hash things out in his mind.

"I did not bring anyone to life, this time," Deloris admits. "In simple terms, Nako. Diana is Artemis's doppelgänger or as I said before Artemis is Diana's Aethoes."

"Oh, I see," Nako said and shakes his little head. "I will never get that right."

"Mr. Nako, I think it is time to repay your kindness by taking a look at the crime scene to figure out who or what stole the statue of Amamet," Diana addresses.

"If I recall correctly, the statue is enormous and it would take a great deal of effort to try and steal it," Deloris said. "Why would anyone want to take it?"

"That is what I have been trying to figure out," Nako assures. "The Middle District Police Department is at an impasse; they have no clue as to how it was taken. It will not hurt for you to take a look. I believe it may have involved the P.I.U. eventually."

CHAPTER SEVEN

The Second Victim

Nako leads the way into the Egyptian exhibit and makes a beeline straight for the Amamet exhibition. Diana quietly discusses the size and location of the missing statue with Deloris as they traverse the hall. The two officers pause as the curator approaches the security bots and punches in a code to playback a video. A miniature holographic image of the exhibition shows the statue sitting in place. Several moments later the hologram goes blank for a few seconds and upon its return shows that the statue is gone. Deloris's features reflect both confusion and surprise as she requests that the footage plays again, this time slowing it down to nearly a frame-by-frame relay. The last frame before it blanks out barely shows a large hand reaching for the camera.

Diana carefully approaches the space of the exhibit to examine the floor, ceiling, walls, and items in the area. She keys in on a display case and goes over to see several artifacts from the tomb housed in the glass enclosure. Among the collection is a set of brittle arrows and next to them is an impression in the shape of a strange dagger. The missing artifact draws the attention of both Diana and Artemis.

The dust and the impression hint the item has several serpentine curves with the handle in the shape of a crocodile's head. Nako jumps up onto the display case, startling the observers slightly, and sits down to look inside with a little frown as he notes the missing item. The police missed this important relic when they created their report. Deloris finally joins the group and hones in on the brittle arrows inside the case.

"Those arrows appear to be too short for the bow that they are lying next to," Deloris observes.

"My understanding is that the bow is Egyptian and the arrows are a mixture of two regions," Nako explains. "The arrows were originally found in the sides of the statue but I had them removed when the statue was placed on the floor. It was for aesthetic purposes. I have a catalog of all the items that were recovered from Amamet's tomb in my office."

"Really," Diana frowns. "Artemis said that those arrows are the reason that Amamet stayed in place."

"That means in theory that this statue could have simply walked out of the museum," Deloris remarks. "Given the size and stature of this golem, I would imagine that the other statues in this entire area may have been damaged as it walked away."

"Not to mention the door, the ceiling as well as the exterior wall of the building," Nako adds. "We had to bring her in by opening up the roof."

Diana takes a step back and looks up to study the ceiling. Through the darkness in the shadows, she barely makes out a thin sliver of light. Large, heavy-duty, hinges line the walls as well as every twelve feet of the massive ceiling. There appears to be no indication that the ceiling has moved recently. Diana respectfully requests that Nako demonstrate the moving ceiling so that she could see it in action.

The seraph cat stretches, patting his paws, and hops off the case to strut towards one of the side walls. He sits down and touches his collar causing it to glow slightly and a small musical note to play. A corresponding note from the wall answers as a light blue button illuminates and deep ominous rumbling echoes from above. Deloris stands next to the intern and watches along with her as the ceiling starts to crack as it folds back upon itself opening the exhibit area to the elements of the night. Fifteen minutes later, the ceiling is completely open.

Nako waits a few minutes before he touches his collar again and engages the mechanics to close the ceiling. The hinges squeak and moan as they move the massive plates into place. When the last few plates come together, they make a deafening boom to indicate that everything is back the way it was. Diana and Artemis share a common look of intrigue even as Deloris lowers her brow and rubs her chin thoughtfully.

"I do not remember reading that Amamet could fly," Deloris remarks.

"I'm told that she could jump pretty high, however, she would not clear the sides of the museum," Diana informs. "The walls do not indicate that she climbed."

"Let's go to my office," Nako suggests. "Perhaps I can persuade some of the museum's neighbors to provide security footage from around the block so that we can search for unusual or strange activities before and after the statue disappeared."

"Give us a minute, Nako," Deloris requests as she sees that the intern is distracted.

Nako tilts his head curiously as he turns to see Diana approaching the wall of a replica inscription that is found in Amamet's tomb. On the left of the drawing is a woman bending down in front of a child. She appears to be speaking to her. Strange Egyptian symbols above represent either a name or title of the illustrated individuals. Continuing across the wall, the illustrations show the girl walking into a strange situation of two monsters.

One of the monsters has a whip and is wearing a spiked collar while the other is wearing a leash somehow attached to its back. The monster with the collar is holding the end of the leash as red drops of saliva fall from their mouths. Symbols representing their names or titles are also above their heads. As the scene continues, they see the little girl chained to a strange arch and another woman holding a serpentine dagger standing in front of her. Next to the second woman are two men, one holding an orb and the other holding a bowl full of liquids.

The narration continues with the little girl marching into the orb which is presented to Amamet. The last scene of the wall shows the first woman that spoke to the little girl being attacked by the monsters. The bowl of liquid is now empty as the second woman and her entourage watch the torment of the first woman. Long and detailed Egyptian writing separates the two scenes explaining what is happening.

"Can anyone read Egyptian?" Diana asks.

"I have an Egyptologist that is caretaker of the Museum of Past Modern History's Cairo branch," Nako offers. "We can contact her when we get to my office. She should still be awake."

"Good deal," Diana said.

The sound of evil laughter fills the silence causing Nako to jump a good foot into the air, landing with his fur on end and his tail raised high. Diana lifts a spear that is leaning against the wall closest to her as Artemis turns with bow in hand, an arrow notched and aimed at the origin of the sound. The laughter comes again is followed by the sound effects of thunder and lightning. Deloris simply smiles when she notices that she is now a target and politely pulls out her phone orb. It levitates as it once again resounds the effects and glows a little bit.

"It's only a phone call, please put your weapons away," Deloris assures as she activates the orb. "This is Deloris..."

"Deloris, I am glad that I have finally reached you. This is Lawson," the commissioner said as a miniature holographic image of his likeness floats above the phone orb.

"Diana and I caught wind of a strange case involving Amamet," Deloris informs. "We are at the Museum of Past

Modern History and it is possible that there is some interference in the building."

"Diana is there with you? This is perfect," Lawson interrupts. "I need both of you to come down to Morstone University ASAP. Same location as before, there is another victim."

"Seriously, the same circumstances as the first?" Deloris inquires.

"Just come down and take a look at the scene, we have not got that much time," Lawson emphasizes.

"Then we are on our way," Deloris said and hangs up the phone.

"There was another party tonight and I was supposed to meet Raquel there," Diana recollects. She then turns towards the wall briefly and takes in the scene once more.

"It looks as if you need to get to the college in a hurry," Nako said as he sits down in front of the two ladies. "You can borrow my limousine to get you there safely and swiftly. It has an incognito mode specifically designed to avoid the traffic police."

"You're very kind Nako," Deloris accepts the gift. "Diana, let's go."

"Artemis said that there is a faster way," Diana informs. "It has something to do with my awakening abilities."

"What sort of abilities are we talking about?" Deloris asks slowly.

"She said that it is better to demonstrate them than to explain them," Diana relays and shakes her head slightly. "I'm not sure I'm ready for surprises like this."

"It sounds as if Lawson needs you there sooner rather than later," Nako reasons. "I might not be an expert on an Aethoes, however, I do not think that Artemis would have you do something that could potentially harm the both of you."

"This is true," Deloris acknowledges. "What is it that you need to do to demonstrate this ability, Diana?"

"Follow me," Diana surrenders and retraces her steps back towards the ancient Greek exhibit.

"You and Diana get to the University anyway that you can," Nako said to his guest. "I will see if I can get my Egyptian expert and call you later on with the translation of the wall."

"Thank you, Nako," Deloris acknowledges the curator. "We will return to finish this investigation once we are done with this emergency."

Nako grins brightly as Deloris bends down and scratches behind his ears before she trails after Diana. The curator then shuffles back to his office as Deloris turns the corner. Diana pauses in front of the giant statue of Artemis and quietly awaits the senior officer to arrive. The statue gives off a soft glow before Artemis herself seems to walk right out of its leg. The Aethoes folds her arms and has a cocky smile upon her face as she scans her mortal doppelgänger and then turns back toward the statue.

Diana's body starts to glow much too the young woman's surprise. The glow spreads from her body and also surrounds Deloris and brightens quickly. The vampire hisses at the sudden glow and flash of light. As suddenly as it brightened, the light dies down and the two find themselves standing in front of a smaller statue of the same deity. Diana reels back from the sudden rush of energy yet other than a small tingle she feels no other ill effects. Deloris takes in the new surroundings with a frown as she notices the windows as well as the red and blue illuminations reflecting through them.

"Where are we?" Deloris asks.

"I..." Diana mumbles and takes a look around. "We are in the museum part of Morstone U. library."

"It appears that traveling with you will become faster at least," Deloris said with good humor as she faces the intern. "Well now, whatever your Aethoes did to you has made you taller. You and I are now seeing eye to eye."

"Is that why my head is spinning?" Diana asks and sits down upon the ground to hold her steadily throbbing noggin.

"Unfortunately, we cannot take much time for you to gain control of your dizziness," Deloris says. "Lawson is expecting us at the Alpha Norma Sigma house."

"All right," Diana relinquishes as she gets back on her feet. "The party that I mentioned at the museum, I will explain what I know once we get to Lawson."

"That would be appropriate," Deloris agrees.

"If we go through the Aligon exhibit, it exits closes to our destination," Diana informs and takes the lead down the hall mentioned. Deloris follows the intern and quickly finds that she must increase her pace to keep up.

There are no robotic tour guides to chastise her nor are there any museum visitors at this time of night. Diana rushes down the long hall and forces the doors to open in order to exit the building, inadvertently knocking them off their hinges. In a few short strides, she reaches a comfortable running speed and heads straight for the fraternity house. Deloris exits the museum through the broken door and quickly knows that she is unable to catch up with the intern.

The vampiress takes a few steps forward and transforms into a large Eurasian Eagleowl, quickly taking to the skies towards her destination. The presence of the media is no surprise as Diana skillfully dodges through them easily avoiding the questions and fury surrounding this new case. She reaches the Alpha Norma Sigma house as Lawson takes out a stick of gum and places it in his mouth. Diana slides to a stop and stands at attention with a professional salute as the dust settles behind her.

"That was fast, did you run all the way here from the Museum of Past Modern History?" Lawson asks.

"No sir," Diana answers respectfully. "We somehow teleported from the museum at the city's center to Morstone's museum. With respect, I am still wrapping my head around the events and will explain more once I ponder the information."

"Glad to see you growing," Lawson dismisses. "Where is Deloris?"

"I thought she was right behind me," Diana admits as she turns back to study her path.

A fleeting shadow flutters through a few of the media lights as the eagle-owl circles around. The bird then swoops down and rears up as Deloris changes back to her original form. The senior officer dusts off her uniform and then stands at attention to salute the commissioner. The media rushes forward only to hit an invisible barrier between them and the P.I.U. officers. Diana, hearing the strange noise behind her, turns to see several of the reporters beating on a barely visible shield that arcs into the sky. The intern arches an eyebrow in curiosity as she turns towards her senior officer. Deloris simply smirks and gives a side glance to the young woman then returns her gaze back to Lawson.

"Reporting for duty sir," Deloris acknowledges. "We came as quickly as possible. Did Diana explain to you our mode of transportation?"

"I'm letting her figure it out before she explains it to me," Lawson admits. "Tonight's victim is different than the first. You will see what I mean when we get up there. I respectfully asked that the family leave her in place until your arrival. They are cooperative."

"Sir," Diana addresses. "There was another party at this location. My understanding is that it was for celebrating a union between future newlyweds. I was invited."

"Newlyweds," Lawson interrupts and nods to the left. "Would one of them be the young woman sitting with the campus emergency squad?"

Both Diana and Deloris look over towards the long red and silver hovercar to see a young woman crying and shaking as she is comforted by one of the staff members. As they study the scene Lawson admits that he did not get a complete story from the distraught woman. She claims that everything is a blur and happened so fast that she is unable to provide any details right now. Not too far from the emergency squad are all the frat brothers standing and staring at their home, a few of them visibly upset that they could not go back in.

Diana takes in both scenes and notices that the frat brother leader is missing among the ranks. Next to the emergency squad's vehicle stand two security robots keeping everyone at bay. Between them is the supposed murderer of the second victim. A little old lady, her hair is in a bun and she is wearing a Hawaiian print dress with matching glasses. Diana frowns as she recognizes the teacher from the Criminal Minds class.

"What is Ms. Cummins doing here?" Diana inquires.

"I will explain that once we clear the scene," Lawson responds. "Do you recognize the young woman who is crying?"

"Yes, her name is Laurie," Diana answers. "She is the bride to be and hostess of this party. If she is here, where is Raquel?"

"Follow me," Lawson said as he turns and walks into the house.

The lights from the cameras flicker and flash as Deloris trails after Lawson. Diana hesitates briefly as she focuses on Laurie. Although the young woman is crying, she did not appear to have true emotion with it. Deloris calls to the intern breaking Diana's concentration as she follows the senior officer into the frat house. The door closes behind them with a gentle click and the first thing that hits Deloris is the smell of fresh blood. She shakes her head and quickly scans the area to see that the substance is not on the walls, ceiling, or floors.

Deloris closes her eyes briefly in order to calm her instincts as she exhales slowly. Diana walks past the senior officer and also takes in the condition of the foyer. The chandelier hanging above them is brand new as is the carpet. The walls are freshly painted and devoid of all wallpaper. Whatever furniture that once stood in the foyer is now gone. Diana carefully peeks into the kitchen and notices that it is newly renovated with cabinets, appliances, paint, and flooring.

"Are you all right Deloris?" Lawson inquires as he takes note of his officer's breathing pattern.

"Give me a moment," Deloris says. "Luckily I did have that snack from Albert's Place earlier this evening."

"Oh, it gets worse," Lawson guarantees. "Let's get upstairs so that we can get her to the hospital."

"Not what I need tonight," Deloris mumbles as she watches Lawson ascend the stairs.

"This is not right," Diana whispers as she approaches the wall.

The paint on the wall is barely dry. She reaches to touch it and then smears it between her fingers. The texture is foreign, almost sandy, and stains her fingers a strange red color. Diana wipes her hand on her pant leg and takes a few steps back. She glances at her Aethoes as they converse in an ancient dialog. Artemis focuses on the wall; there is someone or something powerful blocking or hiding just beyond it. She decides that who or whatever is hiding is not worth bringing down the entire structure to get to, at least for now.

"Are you ready to go upstairs now?" Deloris inquires.

"Yes ma'am," Diana says.

The stairs squeak and moan as the two slowly ascends into the ominously dark hall. Diana hesitates and looks around as if to verify that it is the same hall they traversed during the first incident. Deloris places a hand upon her hip and looks around as she feels a cold and very unfriendly presence glaring at them from the darkness. Both look up and notices that the ceiling is painted over with the same substance that is on the walls downstairs. They take a step into the darkness only for Deloris to hesitate as the scent of blood smacks her harshly. Diana moves away from the senior officer when she detects the quick and sudden change in her demeanor. The intern glances over at her Aethoes to see that Artemis has notched an arrow and is aiming for Deloris's chest.

"I'm not sure who to tell to calm down," Diana says her utmost thought.

"Let's get through this and out of here as quickly as we can," Deloris manages as she once again calms her instincts. "If we tally much longer I may do something that I will not live to regret."

"Yes ma'am," Diana nods and turns to see Lawson standing not too far from their location.

"You both are taking a long time so I came to see what is going on," Lawson said and focuses on his senior officer. "Deloris, you have to give me at least fifteen minutes before you vamp out on me."

"Considering that the only two victims available to me are you and the intern, I will restrain myself or make a hasty retreat if I have to before I attack either of you," Deloris assures.

"Glad to know that neither of us is on the menu," Lawson quips.

The trio continues down the hall with Lawson positioning himself between the vampiress in the intern just in case Deloris loses control. Diana pauses at the room were the first victim was found and frowns when Lawson carries on his way. She catches up to them in time to hear Deloris explain to the commissioner that the room they are approaching is where a frat brother disappeared into during her investigation of Morstone from this afternoon. Diana bends down to examine the floor as Deloris completes her explanation. She touches a dark spot in the carpet in the shape of a human footprint that has dried over time. Diana stands up as Lawson approaches the door.

"I asked the family if we could keep the victim here while you two are en route so that we can complete a thorough investigation. We have forty-five minutes in total together all the information we need," Lawson explains then glances at his senior officer. "With your current condition, Deloris, I would say less than fifteen minutes now. Are you ready?"

"I will manage," Deloris assures.

"I'm ready," Diana says with confidence.

Lawson takes out a handkerchief and uses it to grasp the door handle and turn it. The item squeaks in protest in the door groans as it opens, presenting a dark room to those in the hall. Diana gags at the strong smell of blood that permeates from the room then swears when she hears Deloris makes some strange animal-like sound. The senior officer's whole body is shaking as she battles for control. Once she regains it she exhales and nods to her companions that she is okay for right now.

Lawson looks Deloris in the eyes and notices that they are changing from the emerald green of her calm state to a dangerous blood orange color. Taking a chance, the commissioner walks into the room first and claps twice. The lights pop on immediately to reveal a disheveled room. The curtains are torn down from the windows in the carpet is ripped in various places around the area. The walls are darkened by either fire or a chemical compound with holes in the drywall in a random pattern. Smaller furniture pieces are destroyed and splintered around the entire area.

The bed did not escape the destruction as three of its posts are missing. The sheets and the mattress are torn to shreds and left very little area for the victim to lie upon. It is no surprise that the victim is another woman, her clothing is torn and tattered into nothing but rags and mixes with the other material around the room. She is nude and twisted oddly as if someone shook her like a doll before tossing her upon the bed. Her hair is a mess with many spots rip out of her scalp. Deep cut marks upon her naked body leak with blood and dangerous infection. A pool of blood gathers under her expose hips and is growing by the minutes as she lays there. Unlike the last woman, this one is definitely a victim of sexual assault. Who or whatever attacked her used a sharp object and did a whole lot of damage. Diana walks into the room and freezes when she sees the victim upon the bed.

"Raquel!" Diana exclaims in shock.

"My understanding is that they found her in this location," Lawson explains as his senior officer enters the room. "The old lady that you call Ms. Cummins was also found in this room with a sharp object in her hands and covered in the victim's blood."

"Ms. Cummins is a wildly and crafty old woman, but she is human," Deloris informs. "From my observation, she does not have the strength to overpower a young woman athlete such as the victim easily."

"My experience with Ms. Cummins is that she has a strange way of teaching her class in this would be the next step in her deranged mind," Diana said after taking in the situation. "But it does not make sense."

"Does it ever?" Lawson challenges. "Let's get our investigation done."

Lawson pulls out his camera and starts taking pictures of the entire room being mindful to photograph the areas surrounding the victim. Deloris approaches the bed carefully in order to get a better look at the victim's wounds. As she looks about she spots the bloodied footprint of a man. Diana takes one step towards the bed and hesitates when she senses the approach of another person. She turns as the door opens and in a split second the man that enters finds himself being strangled by the intern.

Deloris looks up and Lawson turns around when they hear the man's yelp of surprise or pain. Beryl coughs and gasps for air as Diana's grip tightens around his neck. She is actually holding him with one hand while the other one is at her side and gripped as if she is holding a sharp object. Deloris is the first to shake off her surprise and quickly approaches the intern.

"Diana, let the man go. His life is not worth a prison term worse than death," Deloris coaxes as she places a hand upon the arm that held Beryl.

"Not until this bastard answers a few questions," Diana grinds out.

"He's not going to answer any questions if he is dead," Lawson observes.

"This is true and he is escorting the emergency unit to this location," Deloris nods towards the small group of people with the intruder. "I do not want to get physical, Diana. There is too much blood here for me to do that."

Diana thinks about the conversation briefly and with convincing from Artemis decides to let the man go. The intern lets out a sound of frustration as she drops him and storms over to the window to look out. Beryl coughs and rubs his throat a little as the emergency unit enters the room. The crew quickly gathers up Raquel and takes her out of the room in order to get her to the hospital. Deloris remains standing in front of Beryl as Artemis goes to talk to her mortal doppelgänger and discuss what happened. Lawson scowls at the entire scene as Beryl assures the emergency unit that he is fine and gets to his feet. The young man takes one look at Deloris, swears, and jumps back away from the vampiress. She simply gives him a very cold, calculated, smile.

"What the hell just happened?" Lawson inquires his utmost question.

"Full disclosure of the situation to be provided once we are outside of mixed company, sir," Deloris offers as she faces the commissioner and salutes.

"Not an answer I want but I will take it," Lawson admits. "And what about you, Diana? Are you better now?"

"Yes sir, I am," Diana assures, turning to the room.

"Good," Lawson said and turns his attention to the intruder. "Beryl, this is the second time you intruded on our investigation. Why are you doing so this time?"

"I did so for Laurie's sake," Beryl explains. "Raquel is her good friend and bridesmaid. I wanted to make sure that she survives to attend the now postponed wedding."

"Any idea as to the timeframe that the victim was attacked," Lawson inquires.

"I left the party to go to the store and pick up more refreshments," Beryl said. "When I left, Raquel was alive and well. When I got back the police are bringing out Ms. Cummins in handcuffs."

"Do you have any witnesses to put you at the store during this unfortunate event," Lawson interrogates.

"I have this store receipt," Beryl hands the document to the commissioner. "The cashier that handed it to me is now off work and the store is closed. I'm sure you know that Emeral is a novelty store run by a family of immigrants and does not use technology as we do."

"I see," Lawson reads the receipt, taking note of the time. "Very well, let's go ladies."

"Yes sir," both Diana and Deloris salute before they march out of the room.

"You may want to retain a lawyer, Beryl, despite being good friends with the bride and groom," Lawson advises then leaves the room as well.

The walk back through the frat house is well lit further showing the detail of cleaning done to present the residence in an acceptable manner for the party. The heavy voices of men indicate that the frat brothers are back in the their home. The odor of blood within the house remains as the officers travel down the stairs. Deloris continues a healthy stride until she exits the building and walks away from it a few paces. Diana pauses and watches the fraternity brothers as they explore their surroundings. She notices them congregating near the strange area she noted earlier in the investigation. Lawson taps the intern on her shoulder and nods towards the exit.

Taking the hint, Diana follows the commissioner out of the house and into the night. The throngs of media are still there taking pictures and speculating their reports to their vast audience. By now, a group of college students is also assembling around the house to find out what is going on. Lawson goes over to Deloris and taps her gently on the shoulder to gain her attention. The senior officer turns and nods, she is okay now.

"Now that we are all together and outside," Lawson says, "will you two explain to me what is going on?"

"Do you remember when I told you that Diana has a supernatural connection to a being that I titled an Aethoes?" Deloris reiterates.

"You told me about a connection or something like that," Lawson agrees.

"After suffering a few power surges and coming to terms with a frightening memory, I finally reconnected with my Aethoes," Diana explains.

"Let's start with something simple like telling me what the hell is an Aethoes," Lawson requests.

"In its simplest form of explanation," Deloris illuminates, "an Aethoes is an immortal being of ancient origin that is linked to a mortal doppelgänger of themselves."

"Okay," Lawson acknowledges. "Besides Diana, how many other of these immortal beings of ancient origin doppelgängers are there hanging around?"

"So far the only ones that I've met are part of Diana's family," Deloris admits.

"My understanding is that every relative in my family is linked to an Aethoes to include a group of cousins that live in the Celtic district," Diana reveals.

"More on that after I've sat down and digested the information that you provided," Lawson politely interrupts. "Just tell me this, should I be ready for explosions or something of that nature in the near future?"

"Oh no," Deloris waves that concern away. "She's already gone through that stage prior to the permanent link she has right now."

"Very well," Lawson accepts the explanation and hands Diana his camera. "I am going to go over and talk to Ms. Cummins. Diana, I want you to take a look at these pictures and compare it to what you may have seen prior to going rogue. We will discuss them as we travel back to the office. Deloris, come with me."

"Yes sir," Diana salutes and accepts the item.

The ambulance turns on its lights and gently nudges its way through the media crowd in order to take the victim to the on campus hospital. Lawson notices that the police department is still trying to interview Laurie even though she is crying on the shoulder of her fiancé. Deloris focuses on Wyliam for a short moment and scowls at his almost rehearsed behavior. Lawson also takes in the scene and decides the best person to talk to at this moment is the police's suspect. As they approach Ms. Cummins, they notice that she still has blood on her arm and hand. Her loud print clothing is torn in two places and she did not have her glasses on.

"Ms. Cummins, I am Commissioner Lawson Trunic, P.I.U.," Lawson addresses as he pulls his badge. "My understanding is that you've already met my senior officer Deloris Matox."

"I have," Ms. Cummins acknowledges. "Your second officer, Diana Hunter, is a student of mine and so I have met the whole team."

"Very observant," Lawson complements. "We have a few questions for you about tonight."

"Ask away," the old woman offers as she focuses on the P.I.U. officers.

"Did you know the victim?" Deloris inquires.

"I do know the victim, she was a former student. She thought I was crazy but that's okay a lot of people do," Ms. Cummins informs as she shifts to become more comfortable. "I did not assault her but on the contrary, I was trying to save her life."

"Can you tell me the circumstances leading up to when you discovered the victim?" Lawson requests.

"I was informed by one of my other students that there was going to be a wedding party at the Alpha Norma Sigma fraternity house and that everyone is invited," Ms. Cummins answers. "So, I came. When I got here all I saw was an empty house so I explored to find out if I missed the party. What I discovered is the victim bleeding profusely so I tried to stop the bleeding unsuccessfully. I left the room to find something to help stop the bleeding when someone tackled me and tied me up. Did I scream and shout profanities? Oh, you bet your bottom dollar I did. Then I was arrested and here I am."

"During the last part of your explanation, did you get a good look at the person that tackled you?" Deloris asks.

"I saw him after the police took me away," Ms. Cummins said.

"Can you identify him?" Lawson requests.

"Ms. Matox already knows the answer," Ms. Cummins informs. "As I said before, it is literally written on the walls."

"Sir, we would have to secure a warrant in order to study that artifact here at the school," Deloris reasons. "And I can almost guarantee you that the school superintendent will not let us in there freely. However, there is a reasonable replica of the very wall at the Museum of Past Modern History."

"Then I guess we will be visiting Nako after this," Lawson puts his notebook away. "Thank you, Ms. Cummins, for your cooperation."

"The only thing I'm asking for in exchange is that you free those lost souls that are trapped in that evil house," Ms. Cummins requests.

A large security robot lumbers over and forcefully requests that the two P.I.U. officers leave the very dangerous fugitive alone. Lawson wisely holds his tongue as he turns and walks away with Deloris in tow. The media is all but gone thanks to the aggressive robots as any observers are pushed back by the security forces.

Diana is now sitting on a bench a short distance from the frat house and pouring over the photographs that Lawson had taken. Artemis is sitting next to her also looking over the pictures and pointing out a few unusual items that the camera's eye has captured. The intern looks up and stands up to salute her returning seniors as she relinquishes the camera back to the commissioner. Deloris takes her turn to review the pictures as Lawson takes out a remote and pushes a button. A waiting police sedan lights up, rises off the ground and hovers over to the group. The doors open to allow the officers to enter. Once they are inside, the doors close in the sedan glides to the nearest exit.

"Diana, do you have class tomorrow?" Lawson inquires of the young woman sitting across from him.

"Yes sir, starting with Basic Paranormal taught by Mr. Murphy," Diana answers.

"I need you to skip a day, I will set it all straight with your uncle. He sent me an email that I need to reply to anyway," Lawson admits. "Did you have a chance to study the pictures?"

"I looked through about half of them," Diana says. "I am still a little shaken from the night's events to concentrate on them fully."

"I think the whole day is catching up with you," Lawson observes. "So instead of discussing the pictures let's discuss what you and Deloris have discovered during your individual researches and investigations."

The sedan picks up speed as it glides up a ramp to the freeway heading into downtown Middle District. Diana goes first with her description as she recalls her findings during her computer research of the Alpha Norma Sigma fraternity.

The original name of the group was the Beta Cosmos which was changed due to a link to a dark past. She describes the murder linked to the group of the past and the necklace they found belongs to that long-forgotten victim. Diana admits that the young lady link to the Beta Cosmos fraternity has the same last name as the current victim, Raquel von Burton. As she tried to dive deeper into her investigation, and old newspaper article about Amamet came up in the computer went blank.

"Looking back, I cannot truly say that it was a power outage or if my newly awakened capabilities caused the power to go out," Diana admits.

"By about then, the two young ladies arrived and I sent you with them," Lawson recollects. "Did you find out anything from observing them?"

"What I found out is slightly strange," Diana answers. "Laurie has a fascination with the new exhibit and Raquel is terrified of her. I also saw that Laurie's fiancé, Wyliam, appeared stunned at the mentioning of a wedding. As if it is the first time he has heard this news."

"That sounds unbecoming of a future husband," Lawson sits back as he takes in the information. "Anything else that you observed?"

"Raquel was a bully type in high school and not afraid of anyone," Diana said as she digs into her memory. "On three separate occasions, I have seen her recoil in fear when Laurie gives her a single look. To me, that is very uncharacteristic of Raquel."

"Considering she almost had a confrontation with me, I can see your concern," Deloris recalls. "She was very protective of you after your first encounter."

"Willing to go toe to toe with a vampire yet cowering at the sight of a former cheerleader," Lawson muses and shakes his head. "There is definitely something more there than meets the eye. Either that or for some reason Laurie appears to be more of a threat than you, Deloris."

"I've not studied Laurie to see whether or not she is a threat," Deloris admits. "However, my investigation into Beryl in the Alpha Norma Sigma fraternity on campus is almost as strange."

The sedan whips around a ninety degrees curve at full speed and then dive straight down into an express tunnel all while the passengers remain comfortably seated and unaware of the variations in the road. Lights flicker over the slick black hull as Deloris explains her strange encounters at the University starting with the empty classrooms. That did not alarm her more so than the empty teacher's lounge that seems to have been abandoned for many years. Deloris carefully chose her words as she explains the encounter with the superintendent, Dr. Pikeys.

It is very apparent that any mentioning of Beryl in a negative way highly upsets the woman. Deloris assures that the only thing they did is exchange harsh words at each other to which Lawson inwardly expresses doubt. The senior officer continues her explanation by revealing that she did make it to the fraternity house undetected. All the brothers at that time were away in classes and she made it all the way up to Beryl's room.

"There was a mural of naked women on the ceiling in the halls at the time, but now it is gone," Deloris explains. "A mixture of Egyptian and Greek symbols was among the drawings. Once I was in his room I noticed that there were tickets to the opening of Amamet's exhibit. One for each member of the fraternity."

"That's a whole lot of money that a college student really should not have," Lawson points out. "Did you ever find Theresa?"

"I did find her, she is Ms. Cummins," Deloris informs. "She claims it is her sister's name but Ms. Cummins is a very strange lady and I believe she is haunted deeply by her past."

"Interesting," Lawson puzzles through the information. "What is this wall that she mentioned to you?"

"It is a stripped-down version of the one at the Museum of Past Modern History," Deloris said. "Maybe we should stop by and study it before we get to the precinct."

"You and I will be going to the museum. As far as the intern, I think we will drop her off for the night," Lawson determines. "You had a busy day Diana, and I think you need to rest."

"I am willing to go with you especially to help solve this case," Diana retorts.

"No, Lawson is correct about your need to rest. Not only from your experiences this evening but from the whole day," Deloris says wisely.

"Yes ma'am," Diana relents, figuring it is best not to argue with either of them tonight.

Moments later the police sedan slows down as it pulls up quietly to the curb of the apartment complex. The door pops open and Diana leaves the sedan as Lawson wishes her a good night and he will see her bright and early tomorrow morning. The door to the sedan closes once Diana clears it and she grumbles that bright and early is exactly three hours from now. Artemis appears next to the intern and places a sympathetic hand upon her shoulder as the two turn and walk into the complex.

The door to the apartment closes quietly as Diana leans against it and turns the lock to secure it for the night. She takes a deep breath in and slowly lets it out, the entire day, as well as the night of events, are catching up to her. Topping it all off is the emotional roller coaster in her dream as well as finding someone she knew in the same predicament as the first night's victim. Taking another breath, Diana finally leaves the door and sits on the couch next to her Aethoes.

A few minutes later, Diana is curled up in a corner of the couch with her head upon the arm of the comfortable piece of furniture, snoozing. Artemis stands up and carefully stretches out her mortal doppelgänger and places a blanket over her. She then sits down in the oversized chair that Melody put back in place and curls up herself taking only a few moments until she too falls into slumber.

CHAPTER EIGHT

Answering the Riddle

The lights burn brightly to assist the rising sun in illuminating the dark and silent office. Voices echo from down the hall signifying the change in shifts as the police department swaps out their staff for the day. Diana stands and does a mighty stretch to loosen tight muscles from her long sit in her chair. She managed to get only about two and a half hours of sleep before a nightmare about Amamet awakened both she and her Aethoes into full alertness. The nightmare was so vivid that Artemis even pulled her weapon and searched the empty apartment for the source of terror. Unable to go back to sleep and noting the time they decided to head into the office.

Diana relaxes her stretch and goes to stand next to Artemis as they both scan the area outside of the window watching the traffic buildup. The computer in front of Diana's desk suddenly beeps to life catching the attention of both of them. The intern turns fully to watch the monitor and keyboard suddenly appear and invisible fingers type upon the keys highlighting where they struck. A deep ominous feeling catches the attention of both Diana and Artemis as they turn their attention to the entrance of the office.

They focus completely on the door as light footsteps echo within the halls beyond and the door itself opens with a groan. Artemis nods and calmly leans against the wall as Diana tries to figure out if she is strong enough to face the dark presence heading their way. The intern turns quickly to her Aethoes when Artemis tells her the identity of the intruder.

"What? That's Deloris?" Diana asks, flabbergasted.

"Well, this is a shock," Deloris says frankly as she rounds the corner. "I did not expect you for a few more hours, Diana."

"Restless night," Diana admits. "Had a nightmare and we both decided to come in here instead of going back to sleep. I only had a half-hour left anyway before I had to show up to work."

"I'd figured you have a restless night. What was this nightmare about?" Deloris sits a cup down on her desk.

"It was about Amamet," Diana explains. "A reoccurring nightmare actually but this time it felt very real."

"It could be that Amamet is taunting you," Deloris hypothesizes. "Any new discoveries?"

"Nothing so far," Diana says and sits down upon the windowsill. "Did you and Lawson get to the museum before Nako left?"

"No, we didn't get in. So, I decided to go home and get some rest myself," Deloris admits as she also sits down at her desk.

"I think I can find the mural at the museum online," Diana suggests. Her attention turns back to the door when it opens again.

"That's Lawson," Deloris whispers to the intern.

"I sense grumpiness," Diana informs quietly.

"Indeed," Deloris grins as she stands next to the intern and the old man rounds the corner. "Commissioner Lawson sir. Buna dimineata."

"Deloris, good morning to you," Lawson responds. "Diana, what the hell are you doing here so early?"

"Still learning my abilities, sir. In doing so I had a few nightmares," Diana explains in short. "I decided to come to work early to get started with the case."

"I've been working this case since I got home last night," Lawson agrees. "Let me get a cup of coffee and I will meet you both in the conference room."

The conference room was a former break room for the entire Middle District Police Department at one time. It has been upgraded with lighting and outdated audiovisual equipment but at least the chairs are comfortable. Lawson walks into the room carrying a large ceramic mug full of a rich dark roast. He sets the coffee down between his two officers and goes to turn on the equipment and get set up before he takes his seat.

The lights dim in the room as the holographic projector finishes warming up and the images of the two victims appear side-by-side. Lawson takes a swig of his coffee then puts it down and explains the similarities he sees in the pictures. The two victims are both positioned the same way upon the bed leading them to believe that the first victim may have also been sexually assaulted. The records that he obtained from the hospital say the contrary.

Further digging into the information, he discovers that the parents were against testing their child for assault. Deloris puts her coffee cup down and then explains the differences in the two pictures. The first victim did not put up much of a fight yet the second victim obviously battled her attackers to the best of her abilities before succumbing to them. Her concern is how the wooden pieces of furniture became splintered so easily.

Diana squirms a little, uncomfortable with the images as the commissioner and senior officer both express their observations. The intern perks up a little when her Aethoes says something to her and points to one of the pictures. In the corner of the first victim's picture is a small image of Amamet yet there was no creature in the compared photo of Raquel. The images flip to two other scenes being compared and now Amamet is in the photo of the second victim and not the first. Diana gawks at the pictures as she sees other images outlined in the blood splatter upon the walls. It looks as if there are two different women in the room with either victim.

Lawson advances the slideshow only for it to stop and flicker back on its own. The second picture of Raquel appears and stops as the first victim's pictures continue to flicker through. Lawson frowns at the behavior of his slideshow and turns to his senior officer. Deloris takes another sip from her coffee cup and looks over his shoulder to the intern. The first victim's pictures suddenly stop once they reach the photograph that Diana is looking for.

The intern stands up and stares at the two pictures, noting that the small image of Amamet is in both pictures and in a similar pose. Lawson turns and tilts his head a little when Diana walks over to the holographic image and takes a look around it from different angles.

"What do you see in the two pictures, Diana?" Lawson inquires.

"I see two things," Diana admits. "In both pictures, there is a grinning Amamet. She is sitting next to the victims in both images. She is also in a pose similar to the Egyptian mural at the museum."

"Are these the only two images that have Amamet in them?" Deloris requests.

"Yes, it is," Diana answers. "However, two other images have something else disturbing about them."

The pictures once again flip until both land on an image that does not have the victim in either case. It shows the corner that is next to the bed in both rooms, distinguished by the missing post in the second crime scene photo. At first, it looks as if there are stripes or bloodstains dripping down the wall. Diana takes out a light pen and starts to connect the different splatters together. Deloris slowly puts down her coffee cup as Lawson leans forward with a sound of awe coming from him.

The image that Diana is drawing is hauntingly similar to the features of Ms. Cummins. In this case, she is a younger woman and her hair is done up in a bun. She does not have the glasses, but the long nose and slightly long chin are very distinguishable. The woman in the photographs appeared to be reaching for the victim, her mouth open and tears of sorrow streaming from her eyes.

"Very interesting," Lawson expresses. "I'll have to go over Ms. Cummins's records to see if she has any kind of supernatural abilities."

"That's not all I saw," Diana admits.

She only changes the scene of the second victim to that of the back corner of the bed next to the window. Another set of splotches line the wall and Diana once again uses her light pen to connect the dots. This time the image comes up as a second woman who seems to be either glaring or smiling at Raquel as she lies upon the bed. This woman is wearing the robe of a priestess complete with a headband of gold with the centerpiece of a crocodile head similar to Amamet. Lawson copies the two images that Diana has drawn and places them side-by-side so that he could compare them. Both ghostly women are the same age and may have been alive at the same time.

"The first images in remorse while the second image seems to be gleeful," Lawson points out. "Do we know who these women are?"

"The second woman appears to be a priestess the first woman I do not know," Deloris observes.

"My understanding from the information provided to me by my Aethoes is that both women are a part of Amamet's cult," Diana explains.

"I am going to contact Nako to see if he has found his Egyptologist," Deloris says as she stands up.

"I'll contact him," Lawson volunteers. "I want you and Diana to go down to the women's prison to see if you can pull more information out of Ms. Cummins. No torture allowed."

"Take all the fun out of it why don't you, sir," Deloris smiles mischievously.

The jails are located in the least desirable parts of Middle District and a full 3 hour sedan ride from the station. Many of the residents of this area either work for the jail system or they were once incarcerated in the various halls. Several people curse, spit or throw bottles at the police hovercar as it carefully winds its way down the street to the women's prison.

The building is a maximum-security operation housing some of the deadliest murderers and criminal minds ever arrested in the galaxy. Large militaristic security bots with two semiautomatic weapons point to the car as it makes its way up the driveway to the main gates. Two more security robots greet the guests by aiming at the car and its passengers as a human guard walks over to the window and orders it lowered.

Deloris kindly shows her badge and that of the intern and watches as the man carefully examines the items then the picture IDs that they also present to him. The human guard frowns as he hands the items back then salutes the car as the window rolls up. The car continues through the gates into the main facility. The large gates then close.

The police car stops at a certain point and opens the door to allow the passengers to exit on the side closest to the building. Diana climbs out first and immediately notices that the atmosphere is heavy and full of tension. The tension increases threefold when Deloris exits the vehicle. The senior officer puts on her shades and looks about at the numerous amounts of prisoners glaring at them from various windows. Seated on top of the building is a giant seventeen cannon robotic gun holding sentry over the entire jail.

Diana whistles a little in admiration when she sees the giant mechanical beast perched on top of the roof. Deloris rolls her shoulder a little as she stands next to the intern and together they walk into the building. Three sets of steel doors close in separate distinctive patterns behind the two once they enter past the threshold. Deloris takes off her shades and places them in her pocket as they approach a glass window with a hole in it. The guard that sits behind the glass scowls deeply at them upon their arrival.

"I am Lt. Commissioner Deloris Matox of the Paranormal Investigation Unit," Deloris introduces. "With me is my officer, Diana Hunter. We are here to see Ms. Cummins per orders of Commissioner Lawson Trunic."

"We have received your request and it has been approved. Please place all your weapons and loose belongings in the hold below," the guard says and opens a door below the window. He pauses when Deloris only places her shades in the hold. "Your standard issued weapons as well."

"As part of the P.I.U., we do not have standard weapons," Deloris explains simply. "All I have on me is my glasses, and we will keep our badges as per protocol 10.3.0.5, section 12." She watches as the man looks up the code.

"Alright," the man says slowly as he finishes reading the section, "you can go inside. You only have a half-hour with the prisoner."

"That's all we need," Deloris smiles at the man as she turns to the large thick steel door.

The hair on the back of Diana's neck stands up as the metal screams against each other in an effort to move the heavy doors. The opening, small at first, slowly widens and reveals a large white room with two robotic guards flanking a distant door, weapons pointed at the floor. Deloris and Diana enter the interview room. The doors grind as they shut behind the two once the officers are in the middle of the room. Diana looks back to see two additional robots hovering next to the entrance with their weapons hanging to the side for right now.

The door on the opposite end of the room shushes open activating the robots next to it. Ms. Cummins, with her hair worn long, is escorted into the room wearing handcuffs and a bright yellow uniform. Flanking her are two burly men armed to the teeth and seems like overkill for the little old lady. They pull out a chair and instruct the prisoner to sit down. Ms. Cummins dutifully obeys the commands as the man and robots train guns on her. The two men slowly back out of the room still aiming their weapons at the little old lady. The door closes and robots once again lower their weapons to their sides.

"Welcome detectives," Ms. Cummins greets. "To what do I owe the honor of being visited by the P.I.U., hmm?"

"I wish to continue the conversation we were having about the first night party and your sister," Deloris answers. "I've brought my intern as she may also have questions for you."

"I see," Cummins sits back slowly. "I can probably answer all of your questions with my recounts but before I do. Diana, you must answer my question. What is it that you hunt, Miss Hunter?”

“Ms. Cummins,” Diana says with some disdain, “I found your question annoying when you first asked it. It is no different this time around.”

“But you do not get answers from me until you answer my question, Miss Hunter,” Ms. Cummins retorts.

“Remind me again why you are asking me this question,” Diana inquires.

“If you will recall, my answer is simply this,” Ms. Cummins focuses upon the young woman’s eyes, “there is something more to you and your name other than the first and the last. If you would but look in the mirror you would see what I mean.”

“Now I understand,” Diana says with a smile and a nod, “Ms. Cummins, I believe your question is more for your curiosity than my abilities.”

“Care to elaborate?” Ms. Cummins retorts.

“I think we can do more than simply elaborate,” Diana says confidently.

The lighting in the room changes to a golden color as Artemis fades into view sitting on a cushion of air next to Diana. Ms. Cummins stares at her former student and the deity seated in front of her. The old woman then takes a look beyond her guests at the robots noting that they did not detect the presence of a fourth person in the room. The old teacher nods to herself as she sits back in her chair with a smile, curiosity satisfied. Deloris restates her question to the incarcerated teacher about the first night party and the event of the past that involved Ms. Cummins’s sister. The old woman leans forward and places her hands in front of her as she stares directly across and begins recalling the events of the past.

"My sister, Agatha Cummins, was, and to some extent still is, involved with a cult that uses the First Night Party as a way of collecting the souls of women and girls for a feast to feed the beast," Ms. Cummins recollects. "One night she described to me what was happening at these events."

The old teacher takes a deep breath as she elaborates on what her sister informed her. She tells her guests that of the characters in the mural on the wall, Agatha would be the one talking to the little girl. The little girl represents the sacrifice to feed the beast. She also tells them that, according to her sister, the girl is a placeholder in the victim is not necessarily a child nor is she a virgin is just that she is female. Agatha feeds the girl a drink or potion of some sort to knock her out and then the victim is tied to a couple of columns.

The unfortunate victim is whipped until she awakens and then tormented until she once again loses consciousness. The head priestess would use the Dagger of Anubis to yank the soul from the body of the victim. The soul is then stored in a strange item with the other victims of the past until they have enough to feed the beast.

The body of the victim is still alive but will appear to be completely lifeless. Usually, the parents or guardians of the victim, if they exist, would believe their loved one is dead. They would pull the plug on the life support machine and perform the ritual burial in accordance with their individual religions.

"How did your sister die?" Deloris inquires.

"This is where it gets good and very, very strange," Ms. Cummins assures.

The old woman sits back and places her cuffed hands in her lap as she recalls the day her sister went from luring victims to becoming a victim herself. It appears that one day Agatha met a young lady with the last name of Hunter. Diana perks up and listens more intensely as the teacher continues to recall this part of the story. Agatha got along with the young woman and they became good friends.

An evening came when the head priestess approached Agatha and informs her that the young woman whose last name is Hunter is to become the next sacrifice. Agatha refused and instead told her young friend to run away as fast as she could from Middle District. The head priestess was furious and as punishment, Agatha was to become the sacrifice.

"My sister's spirit tells me that she was tied to the columns and tormented well beyond any victim prior to herself," Ms. Cummins explains. "She died before the Dagger of Anubis could be used on her. As per the rules of the cult, the head priestess was killed for failing to perform a proper sacrifice."

"During our investigation, we discovered two spirits in the second victim's location," Diana informs. "One of them resembles you and I assume she is your sister."

"Agatha and I are twin sisters so yes if she looks like me than she definitely is my sister," Ms. Cummins admits. "The second spirit that you saw is most likely that of the head priestess."

"Do you have any information as to whom her tormentors were," Deloris asks.

"I will gift to you a little more information than that," Ms. Cummins relinquishes. "My dearly departed sister has informed me that the new high priestess is three to four times crueler than any of the priestesses of the past to include her tormentor. This particular woman likes to use straight torture to render her victims unconscious. She also demands nothing but loyalty. To betray her means that you will be tormented with an attack by two demons of your persuasion, Ms. Matox."

"Really," Deloris arches an eyebrow at that information. "Do you have anyone's name?"

"Between the two of you, you've already met the entire depiction on the wall," Ms. Cummins offers. "Take time to sit down review what you've learned and think about it. You will then know who you seek."

The door from which Ms. Cummins entered opens suddenly as the two guards march in, pointing their guns at the prisoner. The robots do the same as the guards pull the chair back and order the old woman to stand. Ms. Cummins does so without protest and turns to walk out the room back to her awaiting cell. Diana watches with a frown as the door closes in front of her and the robots lower the weapons as the door behind opens up. Deloris stands and instructs the intern to do the same as they turned to leave the interview room.

Diana pauses at the edge of the door and takes a look back once again at the door Ms. Cummins departed through. Artemis frowns then continues to leave the area and is followed by her mortal doppelgänger. The interrogation room's door closes with a deafening tone. Diana meets Deloris in front of the window as the senior officer collects her shades. The two officers are silent as they exit the jail and get into the awaiting police sedan.

Deloris picks up her phone orb and notices that she has a message from the commissioner. She listens to it with a firm nod, placing the item back in its holster as the car glides out of the secure zone and back onto the streets.

"Ms. Cummins provided a lot of information but I somehow think that there are still missing pieces," Diana says. "How her sister died is a little disturbing."

"I think that she may have gotten your family mixed with another family which shares your last name," Deloris speculates. "Lawson wants us to meet him at the museum since we are now done here."

"Yeah, that is a good idea," Diana agrees, "I need to take a good look at that mural again."

"According to our boss, Nako has brought in his Egyptologists," Deloris informs. "This could do one of two things. Solve the mystery are make it deeper."

"I'm voting to solve it," Diana hopes.

The police sedan arrives at the Museum of Past Modern History before the hour and lets the passengers out at the side entrance. A member of the museum's nonmechanical staff greet the two P.I.U. officers and escorts them directly to Nako's office. Deloris enters the room first with the intern following quickly behind. Lawson looks over his shoulder and twists in his chair when he sees the two coming into the room. With him is Nako seated upon his desk as well as a woman they have never seen before.

The stranger is of Middle Eastern descent and turns to smile at the invading party as laughter is reflecting in her sapphire blue eyes. A long main of black hair is braided perfectly and decorated with a golden ribbon. She is wearing jeans and a T-shirt combine with a leather jacket. The woman crosses her legs to reveal a matching pair of leather footwear. The stranger focuses completely on Diana and nods a greeting.

"Hello young lady, I heard you have an Amamet problem," the woman addresses.

"Welcome to the party, ladies. Our guest is Egyptologist, Alys Summers, from the Cairo branch," Lawson introduces. "Alys, these are my officers Deloris Matox and Diana Hunter."

"Alys showed up at my door while I was trying to call her," Nako informs, "then she refuses to tell us anything until you two are here. I'm glad you arrived quickly, the suspense is killing me."

"We also managed to get footage from various security cameras around the block," Lawson says as his officers sit down. "Did you want to review them first or do we go to the mural?"

"My suggestion," Alys offers, "is to review the video footage first then we will talk about the mural."

"That sounds like a plan," Lawson nods.

Nako activates his hologram projector, directing it to an empty part of the office. The familiar scene of the outside of the museum flickers into view and solidifies to an image real enough to touch. It is a miniature version of the building from the camera across the street from the main entrance. Nako switches to a different camera that is on the side of the museum where large delivery vehicles usually dock. A clock displays in the corner of this camera and speeds up until it reaches nine o'clock at night a day prior to the statue's reported missing date.

A thick fog lays heavy around the area as a lone figure walks out of it. The figure is hooded yet it was easy to see that it is a woman and slightly taller than most. Her cloak hides all of her features as she simply lifts her hand and flicks her wrist. The door unlocks and quietly opens allowing the woman to gain access. She is followed by a few dozen hooded men and a second hooded woman.

"Okay freeze it right there," Lawson requests. "The news media reported the statue missing almost exactly 24 hours after that time. How is that possible?"

"The Middle District Police Department recovered a device that creates very real optical illusions at the scene," Nako informs and pulls the device out of his drawer. "Here watch this."

The seraph cat knocks the device off of the desk and it activates. A life-size image of the Amamet statue fills the room. If it was not for the fact that Nako's desk is buried halfway into it, the illusion could easily pass as the real thing. Diana stands up and picks up the small device to examine it.

The item is no bigger than a tube of lipstick that could easily fit into someone's pocket. She deactivates the illusion and carefully places the item back on Nako's desk, pushing it away. She did not want to accidentally destroy it. Alys picks up the item and turns it over to read the inscription on the back with a slight frown. She carefully places the item in her coat pocket to take with them when they leave the room.

"I'm going to start from where we left off," Nako offers as he taps his collar.

The holographic projector starts back up switching to the camera on the inside of the museum and shows the exact moment the door opens up to allow the woman to saunter in. A thick fog rushes in at the same time her entourage does in an attempt to hide them from view. A couple of security bots hurry forward and suddenly malfunction, turn and float away as if they are clearing a false alarm.

The woman continues her way into the museum slowly and is passed by her entourage as they hurry to their destination. The camera that is on the exhibit is the next one up and displays a thick fog wafting in and then a hand disabling the camera. Nako switches to a security camera that is on the hotel perpendicular to the museum and about a block away.

The city lights help illuminate the distant museum as the roof silently opens. Two hooded figures levitate out of the museum followed closely by the floating statue of Amamet. One of the figures dives back into the museum and the roof closes just as silently as it was opened. The figure and the statue levitate a few more feet above the museum then suddenly disappear.

Nako switches the camera back to the warehouse and sees that the entourage accompanying the mysterious figures is all departing. The female figure that had returned into the museum is the last to leave as she closes the door behind her and locks it as the fog lifts. She and the rest of the entourage disappear into various back alleys and streets, blending in with the night.

"Can we go back to where they entered through the back door," Deloris requests.

"Sure," Nako obliges. "Give me one quick second."

The requested scene shows back up after Nako fidgets with some of his controls. The hologram pauses and zooms in on the woman in the hood. Deloris stands up and approaches the image as Nako increases its size to lifelike. The senior officer pauses and looks down at the calf of the figure. The tattoo of an ancient Greek sailing vessel with unique shapes and figurehead is inked on the hooded woman's leg. Deloris takes a step back and stares into the darkened hood of the recorded figure with a very displeased look about her.

"What clue did you find?" Lawson requests.

"Something that I thought I dealt with a long time ago," Deloris answers, cryptically.

"How did you discover that the statue in the display was an illusion, Nako?" Diana asks.

"The device must have run out of power at the time," Nako responses. "I walked past and saw an empty space then I panicked and called the police."

"But where did they take the statue," Diana asks.

"I believe I can help answer that question and many more," Alys offers and stands up. "Let us go to the wall."

Nako hops down off of his desk and shuffles until he is leading the way out of his office. Alys snickers at the cat and lollygags after him followed closely by Lawson. Deloris and Diana stand up then pause when a woman similar to the Egyptologist comes into view as she patiently waits for them at the door.

Instead of the traveling outfit that Alys is wearing, she is wearing a traditional Ancient Egyptian royal dress complete with necklace and golden headband with the figurehead of a cobra. The woman smiles as she nods to the group and Artemis respectfully nods back. Afterward the Egyptian leaves the room following after the departing party. Diana stares after her for a long time as it dawns on her that she is looking at the Aethoes of Alys.

"Does your family have Egyptian roots?" Deloris asks.

"Not that I am aware of," Diana answers truthfully, "although I will make it a point to ask my uncle when I see him."

Alys enters the exhibit area and awaits patiently as her audience files in behind her. Once they are all there, she takes out the optical illusion stick and tosses it on the floor. The image of Amamet fills the space as Alys begins her explanation. She explains that Amamet is a fantastic beast with the hindquarters of a hippopotamus, the shoulders and torso of a lion, topped off with the head of a crocodile.

Alys casually walks around the illusion of the beast as she explains that Amamet's name actually means the devourer. In the past, she would eat those souls that failed to pass their final judgment. However, it is hard to keep a creature such as Amamet sustained or tamed for long. One day this fantastic beast rebelled and devoured any and every soul that she could get her mouth on. Her keeper, Anubis, either refused to stop her or literally could not.

"She was stopped towards the end of one of many catastrophic wars," Alys informs. "The arrows in the case belong to the two archers that put a stop to her rampage. One was Artemis the other one was Pakheth."

"My understanding from my Aethoes is that they did not get along very well," Diana says after feeling a rush of negative energy from Alys's information.

"My guess is because both are wild at heart and have similar tendencies," Alys says with a smile. "Pakheth will cooperate only with those she believes have the same goal that she does. Hence is how Amamet was stopped."

"You said stopped but not killed," Lawson repeats. "So, you're telling me that the statue is real, alive?"

"Yes, she is but she is not awake yet. She still needs to feed. Which leads me to the wall mural," Alys remarks as she walks over to the wall. "My understanding is that you went to talk to an old woman named Ms. Cummins."

"Between the two of us we've talked to her a few times," Deloris agrees. "Her favorite answer is that what we seek is literally written on the walls."

"She is right," Alys agrees. "I should have come here sooner and the girl would not be in as much peril as she is now. Do you recognize any of the figures?"

"Can you tell us with the hieroglyphics are saying above each figure?" Lawson asks.

"Sure, it should help clarify some of what the wily teacher has provided as a statement," Alys relents and turns to the wall. "This is rather gruesome; however, the first woman and the very last are the same and it translates to Captor. The two demons, one dominant and one slave, are really not demons. Above them, it says drinkers of blood."

"Considering there was limited alien contact by species that feast on blood outside of Earth back in those days," Deloris crosses her arms as she stares at the image. "You're telling me that those two are vampires."

"Not necessarily," Alys assures. "Aside from vampires, there are humans that enjoyed the taste of blood. Let me move on before we get into more questions. Of the two gentlemen, the one with the bowl, is called 'the one who holds the bait.' The second man with the ball is the keeper of the souls."

"So the second full-grown woman is a priestess of some sort?" Nako asks.

"Yes, she is the one that feeds Amamet," Alys says. "I forgot the little girl though I think you already know that she represents the victim."

"So why is the Captor being attacked?" Diana inquires.

"Because according to this inscription," Alys touches the wall. "If the Captor fails to bring the victim to feed Amamet. She becomes the victim through torment."

"Interesting," Deloris says. "Taking current circumstances, it is safe to say that Raquel fills the role of the Captor."

"From how you describe her, it's no stretch of the imagination to say that Laurie is in the role of the priestess," Lawson deduces. "I have no doubt that Beryl plays a role on that wall somewhere. Any other players?"

"The little girl, known as the victim, represents all victims of this cult," Alys says to avoid confusion. "My understanding, Diana, is that the Captor was trying to lure you to a couple of parties."

"I am so confused," Diana admits as she holds her head. "My memory of Raquel does not recall her being subservient to Laurie or ever wanting to join any cult. How can things change so rapidly?"

"Laurie's powers of persuasion are not limited to simply verbal or physical abilities," Alys hints. "The high priestess who feeds Amamet has strong metaphysical abilities as well."

"Or just maybe you do not know Raquel as much as you thought you did," Lawson submits sympathetically. "Deloris you look like you're puzzling over something."

"The two 'drinkers of blood' and the two men I am still trying to place them," Deloris admits as she stares at the wall. "In this day and age, I feel that those two creatures are either true vampires or one of many alien races addicted to the blood of earthlings."

"Remember, Ms. Cummins informed you that between the two of you, Deloris and Diana, you have met this entire mural," Alys reminds. "Do not tally on it too long or you will be too late to save Raquel."

"How do we save a soul that is separated from the body?" Diana inquires.

"Retrieve the orb that the keeper is holding," Alys answers. "Take it to the hospital and destroy it in the room that the victim occupies."

"Thank you, Ms. Summers, for this in-depth knowledge of the situation," Lawson says as he shakes the woman's hand. "If you will excuse me, I need to go make a few phone calls."

Lawson exits the exhibit as Nako bats at the illusion generator until it turn off. Alys picks up the item and places it in her pocket once again. She then gives Nako a gentle scratch behind his ears much to his delight. The head curator then saunters away, pleased with the attention provided to him. Alys shakes her head and stands back up, turning to see the two officers still studying the wall.

Diana barely jumps when the Egyptologist quietly arrives next to her to study the wall as well. Deloris muses over the two demons until she notices that the one standing up has a spiked collar around its neck and what appears to be a whip in one of its hands. She recalls the two items hanging in a shadowbox on the wall of Dr. Pikeys's office.

"I wonder if one of those demons is Morstone U's superintendent," Deloris muses. "Then it is logical or even expected that the second one is the rogue vampire."

"I've never met the superintendent of the college," Diana admits. "My understanding is that is best not to meet her. The only rogue vampire that I know is Laurie's supposed fiancé Wyliam."

"I think we are speaking about the same person," Deloris responds. "So, which one is Beryl in which one is an unknown?"

"Do not think too deeply into this mural," Alys warns. "You will become so lost in the details that you miss your mark."

Diana stares after Alys upon hearing the familiar words spoken not too long ago by Ms. Cummins. The Egyptologist nods to the young lady then excuses herself as she leaves the exhibit trailing after her supervisor. Diana watches her leave and then turns to see Artemis talking to the Egyptologist's Aethoes next to the case of artifacts.

Curious, the intern goes over to look inside the case and listen as things are explained to her one at a time. One of the items floats out of the case, through the glass, and levitates in front of Diana. It is a small coin with the figure of a woman kneeling with her arms up. Diana takes the coin from the air and turns it over to read the name, Isis, on the back. Slightly stunned by the information the intern looks up only to see that her Aethoes is the only one standing there.

"She walked away as soon as you took the coin," Deloris informs as she arrives next to the intern. "I had a feeling that Alys is the doppelgänger of Isis."

"I've a feeling that we will be seeing her again in a not-too distant future," Diana predicts.

"Do we have to add clairvoyance to your list of abilities, Diana?" Deloris teases.

"I would not say clairvoyance just a really deep gut feeling," Diana admits. "I think we have done more than enough research. How did you want to proceed from here?"

"Perhaps we should try to figure out where the statue was taken," Deloris says. "That is until Lawson finally gets the warrants that we need to proceed with arresting all parties involved not to mention a thorough search of the Alpha Sigma Norma fraternity house."

"And the woman that stole the statue, you've seemed to have run into her before?" Diana asks.

"I have," Deloris nods. "Thank you for the reminder, I am going to need something to tide me over just in case we run into her. Needless to say, it will be a hell of a battle."

Captured

The next day, the halls of the school bustle with students as they grab books and any supplies they need for their next class. Locker doors slam shut in chaotic harmony all around Diana as she carefully places items in her backpack. She waits until traffic clears a little before closing her locker and shoulders her pack. She turns in time to see Wyliam pause at the edge of the hallway. Diana locks eyes with him briefly before he appears to swear, turn, and briskly walk back the way he'd come.

A number of students file after him in order to get to their appointed studies. Diana shrugs and moseys down the hall artfully avoiding the hurried students so that she does not collide with them. She enters the classroom that actually holds her first class at the school, Basic Paranormal. Diana glances around the room as she notices that she is the only student in the class. She makes a curious sound as she sits down and takes out her schedule.

Diana rolls her eyes when she notices that the classroom number has changed to a different hall. She is about to pick up her backpack when a test paper is slapped down in front of her on the desk. Diana pauses as she takes a look at the ungraded test and scowls as it has an accusation written upon it that she did not care for.

"Miss Hunter, can you explain to me why you cheated on your test?" Murphy inquires, accusingly.

"I do not cheat on tests, Mr. Murphy," Diana corrects, slowly looking up to the teacher. "I took the test using the instruments that you provided."

"No one in Basic Paranormal was able to get a perfect score on my first week's test since I have been teaching at Morstone University," Murphy snaps, interrupting the young woman. "You are the only one in the class with a perfect score."

"As an intern of the Paranormal Investigation Unit, I have more advanced knowledge of paranormal activity than the average beginner," Diana answers simply, getting to her feet to meet the professor eye to eye. "You are out of line to accuse me of cheating on a quiz that you know is way above your student's heads. I pointed that out to you when we first met."

"I do not believe you, not one word," Murphy snarls.

The classroom appears to physically twist upon itself as several strange creatures jump out of various locations all aiming towards Diana. The young woman quickly realizes that Mr. Murphy is sending a full-blown fear wave attack. In fact, the teacher's features warp until they resemble a deadly great white shark.

Diana scoffs as she bore her gaze into the eyes of the attacking professor. The mechanical systems in the room start to either speed up or break down as a wave of electricity wafts off of the young woman. The pupils of Diana's eyes quickly shift to a pristine green as the fear wave is canceled. Mr. Murphy doubles his effort in vain as his victim does not budge or submit to any of the fears that he throws at her.

"As I stated before, Mr. Murphy, your tricks do not work on me," Diana says slowly.

"I see. Since you will not admit it to me, you will defiantly admit it to Dr. Pikeys," Murphy nearly belts. "You are to go to her office at once, do not dally or ignore the order. The last person you want to hunt you down is the superintendent."

"I see," Diana says, purposefully holding back her angry response. "The only reason I am going down there is to clear my record. Then, Mr. Murphy, you will have to explain your accusations."

"You should not use idle threats on me, little girl," Mr. Murphy sneers.

"I do not issue empty threats or promises, old man," Diana retorts.

The temperature in the room rises slightly, unnoticed as both parties continue their impasse across the short distance of the desk. Diana, still glaring into the professor's eyes, lifts up her backpack and shoulders it. Murphy tries a different method of fear attack only for the wave to slap him back. The strength of the slap makes him blink and reel back as he realizes that there is some sort of amplification upon the attack. Diana glances over her shoulder to see Artemis leaning against the wall, giving her a nod.

The young woman grins a little then takes the opportunity to turn and leave the room, carrying the accusative paper with her. Murphy glowers after the young woman as she leaves then angrily slams the door behind her. Diana pauses when she hears the door slams. After a moment, she decides not to go back and reengage the teacher. Taking a deep breath in and out to calm herself, she walks down the hall. Artemis walks with her, quietly discussing the events that happened in the classroom as well as the upcoming meeting. The Aethoes warns her mortal doppelgänger that the superintendent is a lot more powerful than the professor. In fact, she is nearly on par with Deloris in her abilities.

"Seriously," Diana stares at her Aethoes when she receives the information. "I never met the superintendent so safe to say she's a vampire. If she is as powerful as Deloris, she is pretty high on the metaphysical spectrum. I will have to stay on my guard in there."

The hall to the superintendent is dark and bleak with a strong negative energy radiating from the door at the end. Diana hesitates when she reaches the beginning of the hall and stares down at the door, quietly wondering what she is getting herself into. She tears her gaze from the door and focuses on the paintings lining the hallway. All the past superintendents appear to be horrified that she is even thinking of going towards the current school leadership office. Diana looks at the paper and then crosses her arms as she once again stared down at the door. Artemis imitates the stance as they both quietly discuss the odds.

After a moment, Diana rolls her neck and shoulders a little and starts walking into the obvious danger, followed closely by her Aethoes. The door opens and the robotic secretary scans the student once before alerting the superintendent that her appointment has finally arrived. The door to Dr. Pikeys office opens, the woman inside beckoning her appointment to enter.

Diana feels the woman's attempt to claw at her mind and bats it away before she goes into the office. Raine Pikeys is standing and smiles at this latest victim before offering a seat. Diana instead decides to stand in front of the chair, opting to remain on her feet for this meeting. The young woman places the paper in question upon the desk causing the superintendent to smirk.

"Let's see, Diana A. Hunter," Raine Pikeys reads the letter in front of her. "What does the A. stand for?"

"Take a guess," Diana quips.

"Sassy I see," Raine notes then places the paper down. "It seems that you have been cheating on your test. Mr. Murphy's entry exam has never been passed by first-year students in the history of his class at this school. How is it that you passed it and from my understanding, before class ended?"

"I am more advanced than the other students due to my internship," Diana answers simply. "My credentials are in my files."

"I see," Dr. Pikeys smiles a little. "Perhaps you can elaborate. Then again, you don't have to..."

Diana cusses when the chair behind her suddenly slams into the back of her legs forcing her to sit down. She feels a great power wrap around her to keep her seated as it tries to rip through her mind. Diana lets out a sound of frustration as she pushes back at Pikeys. The force of the resistance has the superintendent arching both eyebrows, impressed by the girl's ability.

Diana lets out an angry yell as she frees herself, destroying the chair in the process. The display of strength brings the superintendent to her feet. Pikeys grins at her challenger as she flicks her wrist to send a strong wave of pressure in the young woman's direction. The invisible force strikes Diana, sending her back several feet, yet it does not knock her down. The student swears in annoyance as Pikeys once again tries to rip through her mind.

The superintendent's attack suddenly reverses, slamming into the originator. Pikeys reels back and shakes her head, swearing from the unexpected retaliation. She looks up in time to see that her intended victim now has a visible twin. Artemis places a hand on Diana's shoulder and instructs her mortal doppelgänger to imitate her stance.

Golden light swirls about the room and coagulates around Diana and Artemis. The duo takes a single step forward, turns, and comes back around as if tossing something directly at Pikeys. The golden light explodes towards the superintendent, swirling around itself as it nears the target. Pikeys is caught off guard and crosses her arms to block it as it slams into her, sending her back into her trophy wall. The superintendent lets out a strange bellow of rage as her eyes become blood red and her fangs come into full view. Pikeys flips, bounces off the wall, and sails directly at Diana. The intended target prepares to defend herself.

Artemis simply folds her arms and gathers the golden energy around them forming an arcane shield. Pikeys strikes the shield, is pushed off harshly, and is sent into the wall behind the defenders. Diana faces the wall, preparing for a second bout when Artemis once again touches her shoulder and shakes her head. It is best to get out before Pikeys really gets started. Diana acknowledges the words of wisdom and slowly backs out of the office as Pikeys walks back in via the hole she created. Diana briefly meets the gaze of the superintendent and then closes the door. Pikeys scowls angrily at the young lady's departure then growls as she picks up her phone.

A grove of students fills the halls of the main building as Diana rounds the corner. She shifts her backpack as she continues to the exit purposefully ignoring the look of surprise from Mr. Murphy as she passes his classroom. She barely crosses the threshold to the outside when her phone orb rings and then chimes. Diana pauses and steps to the side to keep from being run over by her fellow students, taking her communication device out of her pocket. She unlocks it and notices that the call is from her uncle requesting an afternoon meeting regarding a letter sent to him by Dr. Pikeys. Diana frowns when she reads the attached letter, noting that the test paper is among the documents sent to her uncle. Diana holds back her topmost thought as she makes an update to her calendar to meet with the one that is funding her education.

"I think I should see Raquel before I leave campus as I have a feeling that once I go I will be banned. Especially after that spat with the superintendent," Diana converses with her Aethoes. "The hospital is about a three-and-a-half-mile hike from here. While we are walking, I do have a few more questions about the link that you and I share."

During the light stroll to the hospital, Diana asks a few simple questions about the past and what to expect out of her awakening abilities. Artemis admits that each iteration of her mortal doppelgänger has different abilities and sometimes it is an enhanced version of the previous. As far as Diana is concerned, they will have to wait and see what else shows up in the next few weeks.

The current link that they share can be more powerful, however, there needs to be a higher level of trust between the two of them. With a full connection, if Diana perishes, so does Artemis. Also with this current link, it is easily broken whereas a full link cannot be broken with the exception of someone or something strong enough to sever it or Artemis herself destroys it. Artemis guarantees that they have not reached Diana's full potential yet.

Diana contemplates the information as they reach their destination about an hour after the skirmish with Dr. Pikeys. The glass entrance shushes as it opens up to allow the visitors access to the building. A guard bot scans Diana once then acknowledges that she has no visible weapons upon her person. The mechanical being seems to ignore Artemis and her weapons. It did not see her.

A second set of doors opens to allow entrance into the main lobby of the hospital. Diana walks into the room, going straight to the information desk. A large hologram of an elderly woman sits in place of a robot or volunteer and greets everyone with an eternal smile. Diana shifts her backpack to her other shoulder and scans the list of patient names scrolling up the wall of light next to the old woman. She frowns a little when she notices that Raquel is not listed among the patients and turns to the greeter.

"Excuse me. I'm looking for Raquel von Burton. Is she still at this hospital?" Diana inquires.

"Please, identify yourself?" the old lady asks politely.

"Diana A. Hunter, authorized intern of the P.I.U.," Diana informs as she digs out her badge and presents it. "I am on official duty."

A blue light shoots from the hologram's eyes and scans the badge then the woman. Diana waits until the blue light disappears to place her badge away. The hologram smiles brightly as a datapad in front of it lights up with the requested information. Diana reads the document, locating Raquel on the fourth floor intensive care unit. The patient's visitors are restricted to family, friends, and the police department at this current time.

Diana thanks the greeter and heads to the open doors of the elevator just down the hall. She enters it and notices that the desired floor is already highlighted as the doors close. A few seconds later they open once again at her destination. Several nurse bots whiz around the space going in and out of patients' rooms to check on them. At the desk sits a seraph cat dressed in a nice hat and small ruffle shirt.

Diana approaches the head nurse and requests permission to see Raquel as per protocol. The seraph cat verifies the young woman's identification then hops to the floor to saunter down the hall, leading the visitors to an isolated room near the back of the unit. Diana exchanges a brief glance with her Aethoes as the small being walks away.

The life-support machine beeps and blips as the door to the room opens. The iron lung moves rhythmically to keep the human body alive. Diana peaks into the room to make sure she is not disturbing anyone then slowly walks in. She carefully approaches the bed as the door quietly closes behind her. Artemis stands next to Diana as they both scan over the victim. Raquel is now clean with a white hospital gown to cover her instead of her torn and tattered clothing. A loving relative has recently combed and braided her hair.

A sheet covers Raquel's lower body to keep her modest and warm in the otherwise cool environment of the hospital. Diana settles her nerves as she slowly lifts the unconscious woman's arm and studies it. There are rope burns as well as whelps up and down the appendage. Diana places the arm back down and takes a step back observing that the whelps also cover her neck and extends up to the victim's cheek. The intern taps the screen located at the base of the bed so that she can study the medical chart as her Aethoes focuses on Raquel's neck.

"Let's see here," Diana types in her credentials and is happy when the screen comes up. "It says that the patient arrived anemically and was given several blood transfusions in order to keep her alive. There was a good amount of internal bleeding and emergency surgery was needed to stop it. She was split on the inside." Diana pauses and looks over to her Aethoes. "Her neck? It did not look broken."

Diana leaves her post to go examine the area Artemis informs her about. She pushes down on the pillow gently to get a better look at the bruises around the victim's collarbone. There are two pin size holes barely seen against Raquel's dark skin located in this area. Concern crosses Diana's features as she once again examines the woman's arms, there are no pin marks on either arm. She examines the other side of the neck and sees that there is no other mark. Diana frowns in thought as she retrieves her phone orb from her backpack and dials the office number.

"Buna dimineata, Diana," Deloris answers as her holographic image appears above the orb. "This is an unexpected phone call, how is your first day back at school?"

"Ma'am," Diana salutes the senior officer. "I had a few run ins and may be expelled, however, that is not why I contacted you. I'm visiting Raquel at the campus hospital and discovered that she has an instance of twin pin size holes in her neck."

"This may correspond with the mural that Alys translated for us yesterday. Are there any more similar marks anywhere on her body," Deloris asks.

"Other than the incident on her neck, I didn't see anything. Wait a minute," Diana answers and stares at Artemis for a moment when she receives more information. "What? Her left thigh has something too? I will trust you on that, Artemis. I'm not going to look at Raquel's inner thigh."

"I will be there soon as I can. Have the head nurse meet me when I arrive," Deloris says. "When I get there, we can discuss why you will be expelled."

"Yes ma'am," Diana salutes and hangs up the phone. "I'll be right back."

Diana puts the phone orb into her backpack and places her belongings that were in the chairs in the corner of the room before she leaves into the hall. Whispers of conversation buzz in the area as nurse bots exchange information with living nurses. Diana dodges the caretakers as she makes her way back down to the triage station. Halfway to her destination, she sees the back of Beryl as he leaves another room and heads down a previously unknown stairway.

Diana makes a curious sound as she goes over to the room to take a look inside. Other than a strangely antique bed, the room is empty. Diana takes a few steps back as she shakes her head sensing something is not right. She turns and bends down to study the floor that leads to the stairway taking note that Beryl did not leave any tracks.

Diana leans her elbows on her knees as she recalls the small holographic mechanism that replaced Amamet at the museum and its demonstration last night. She stands up and goes to look in the room once again this time staring into it. The bed in the room wiggles a little and then returns to a normal state. Diana shakes her head again as she comes to a conclusion.

"Listen to your good sense, girl," Diana scolds herself.

Diana continues her journey to the triage station once again then turns when she is a distance away to look back down the hall. The room is now dark which piques her curiosity. Diana ignores her inquisitiveness as she focuses on her destination. Once there she finds the calico seraph cat busy patting her paws on a large digital keyboard as she takes in her reports for the day. Diana approaches the busy feline and makes the request to her.

The head nurse pauses in her report and pulls up the information on the senior officer of the P.I.U.. Diana explains that there is an issue in Raquel's room and what it is. The head nurse frowns at the news citing that if she had known of the attack, they would have done a victim's kit to find out who or what attacked her. The sexual assault kit came back inconclusive, but the second kit may have yielded a better idea as to whom the suspect would be.

Unfortunately, now that Raquel is all cleaned up and many of her wounds healed it is not possible to get the DNA needed for the kit. Diana acknowledges the small being's frustration and journeys back to Raquel's room as the nurse prepares for Deloris's arrival.

Less than an hour later, the door to Raquel's room opens once more catching the attention of those still present. Diana looks up from her online game and puts her phone orb away as she acknowledges the senior officer of the P.I.U.

Artemis gives a courtesy glance over her shoulder and nods to the intruder then returns her gaze back to the scene outside the window. Deloris nods to the Aethoes and acknowledges the intern as she approaches the victim's bedside. She takes off her shades, causing them to disappear in the red flash as the lead nurse saunters in followed by a robotic assistant. Deloris taps on the screen at the base of the bed to bring up the chart to read it herself. She focuses in on the blood transfusions and the hysterectomy but did not see a mention of a victim's kit other than the one for sexual assault. The head nurse explains that she recently found out about the possible vampire attack.

Deloris half listens to the explanation as she pushes down on the pillow to see the two marks on the left side of Raquel's neck. She then moves back to allow the nurse bot to glide over and remove the sheet. Deloris gently examines the inner thigh of the unconscious woman and sees the puncture wounds that were mentioned in the phone call. She uses two fingers to measure the distance to the holes on the neck and repeated the process on the thigh with a slight nod to herself.

Deloris carefully removes the gown on the victim's upper body and examines the breast. They are bruised but there are no bite marks upon them that she could see. Deloris quietly expresses relief for the news and carefully puts the gown back in place as the nurse pulls the sheet back upon the young woman.

"She was bitten by two different vampires," Deloris informs those in the room with her. "A female bit her on the neck and a male bit her on the thigh. It was not without a fight as far as I can tell, hence all the bruising."

"She didn't stand a chance," Diana concludes sadly. "My guess is that it takes more than two bites to turn a human into a vampire, right?"

"You're correct," Deloris agrees as she faces the intern. "There are four bites and it has to be from the same vampire. Areas to look for a female would be the left side of the neck, the right breast, the left wrist, and the left thigh. Usually, the victim is willing as it is during intimacy."

"I think that counts Raquel out," Diana says.

"When she wakes up, she may have a very deep fear of vampires because of this attack," the head nurse says matter-of-factly.

"Oh yes, it usually happens to victims of such violent attacks," Deloris acknowledges. "If I can get a notification when Miss Raquel von Burton awakens, I would appreciate it. I'd like to make sure that she does not need a reversal."

"I will send you a text when she awakens and whether or not she needs the reversal," the nurse cat offers. "Right now, I need both of you to exit the unit. Visitation hours are limited up here in the I.C.U. Please understand.”

“We understand,” Deloris assures. “Diana let’s go as I need to talk to you about your possibility of being expelled from Morstone University anyway.”

“Yes ma’am,” Diana salutes

The large glass doors shush as they close behind the departing officers. A dark ominous cloud echoes thunder overhead. Diana hails one of the on-campus robotic motorcars to shuttle them to the Expo building. While they are riding, the intern and her Aethoes explain the encounters that occurred during the morning hours.

Diana starts with an explanation of Wyliam’s behavior as he practically avoided her. She informs that which is uncharacteristic of him. She continues with the accusations and unique attack from Prof. Murphy adding that she may have overreacted just slightly. Lastly is the skirmish that she and Artemis had with Dr. Pikeys and that the superintendent tried to claw her way into Diana’s mind.

“Did she try to bite you?” Deloris inquires.

“I think that may have been her next move,” Diana hypothesizes. “However, after Artemis tossed her through a second wall, I was told to back out of the room. Apparently, Pikeys was just getting started.”

“Just getting started you say,” Deloris arches an eyebrow. “I too had a small spat with her prior to our museum visit. What else did she try?”

“Did not get past levitation,” Diana assures. “Artemis tells me that Pikeys is close to you on the metaphysical scale.”

"Now I am intrigued," Deloris says. "When we return to the station, I will have to do a little homework myself."

The doors to the Expo building open silently into a large, dark, empty space. The light source for the entire structure consists of sunlight filtering through the tinted windows. The table and chairs, as well as the temporary cafeteria that once occupied the building, are no longer there. Yellow tape is strung from wall-to-wall with the word caution printed in regular intervals upon it.

A sign directly in front of the visitors advertises a special event to honor the victims from the frat house party murders. The date and time are today at sunset. The location is in the middle of the Expo building. Deloris and Diana quietly discuss the party and the fact that there is no activity from either student or staff in preparation for it.

"I don't get this," Diana says, her voice echoing in the empty hall. "There does not seem to be a sponsor for this event."

"When it comes to large activities such as a memorial it should be orchestrated through the school," Deloris agrees. "Do you have access to the school calendar or should we go to the library to use the systems there?"

"You are in danger," a voice moans from the gloom. The unexpected words cause the visitors to jump slightly and face the darkness.

"Your words are ambiguous," Deloris speaks to the invisible person.

"Can you be more specific on what danger you are referring to?" Diana adds.

Light catches the attention of the visitor as it shimmies out of the darkness of the hall that once led to Ms. Cummins's classroom. It moves slowly for a few feet then hesitates and floats back down the hall. Seconds later, it returns and stretches out slowly to form the figure of a young woman, this time fully intact. Diana recognizes the ghost that she encountered on the first day of classes when she traversed the same hall. Artemis glances around the entire area as if seeking the second entity they crossed paths with on the same day. The grey spirit motions for them to come into the hall. Deloris carefully weighs the odds, remembering the mural on the wall as well as the old teacher's explanation about her sister.

"Do we accept the invite?" Diana inquires.

"Do you feel comfortable with it?" Deloris counters. "Remember, in life, she was the one labeled the Captor."

"I remember," Diana agrees. "I met her on the first day of school. There was a second spirit as well. That one, I believe, is the priestess."

The temperature in the room goes down enough to be noticed as the lighting changes to a deep maroon color. A wave of dangerous energy slams into the trio, nearly pushing them backward. Diana and Artemis shake off the energy as they quickly look about the room. The intern is the first to spot the black shadow forming near the corridor, the grey ghost is gone.

Shrieks of pain and anger echo in the Expo building as the darker spirit finish contorting and condensing until she was fully visible to the onlookers. She is barely recognizable as once being human, her hair tattered and clothing flapping together as shadows continue to swirl about her. Fingers are replaced with talons and the legs no longer a part of the figure. The poltergeist is barely able to close her jaw as drool drips from the moth and oversized pointed teeth. Deloris rolls her neck and shoulders as she faces the specter.

"I know this is a new concept for you. However, I am going to ask you once to leave this realm and travel to your final destination," Deloris says calmly.

"Are you the Keeper of the Dragon's Teeth?" the ghost demands.

"Keeper of the…" Deloris appears stunned from the title then her features changed to that of anger. "No, I am not."

"Then you cannot command me, and you will die!" the ghost shrieks.

"Adu-l," Deloris challenges.

Diana takes a few steps back to stand with her Aethoes as the ghost screams angrily. The spirit charges to her intended target and smacks into a shield. The ghost reverts back to the shadows and surrounds the entire shield, attempting to break it in order to get inside to her prey. Deloris glares into the red eyes of the shadow and uses her shield to squeeze the shadows into a tight box.

The poltergeist yowls as she reforms into the woman and rakes her talons on the invisible barrier in an attempt to free herself. Deloris begins to speak in an ancient language as she casts her incantation below the trapped specter. The floor underneath the ghost lights up with several runes then a black hole opens up, swirling the light around the rim. A shriek of rage and fear exits the trapped ghost as it is sucked downward into the floor. The tunnel then slams shut and Deloris lowers her shield.

"What just happened?" Diana asks then looks over to her Aethoes. "A direct connection to Tartarus? And who is the Keeper of the Dragon's Teeth?"

"Yes, it was a direct connection," Deloris answers. "The Keeper of the Dragon's Teeth was Medea. She was once Princess of Colchis, among other titles. Legends do not tell what happened to Medea, but I know."

"What happened?" Diana asks carefully.

"We need to go see if we can free or interrogate Agatha Cummins," Deloris changes the subject.

Deloris sets course for the darkened hallway as Diana poses the same question to her Aethoes. Artemis admits to not really knowing what happened to Medea only that she disappeared after killing her children. She also advises not to press the question to Deloris at least right now. They will get the answer, in time. Diana frowns at the answer but decides to heed the warning as she follows the senior PIU officer into the darkness.

The hall leading to Ms. Cummins's classroom becomes even more ominous as the sounds of thunder from the storm reach those traversing the path. Diana pauses at the locations that she encountered the ghost before with no luck. She continues on and finally reaches the classroom, catching up to Deloris. Diana looks around and sees that all of the furniture is now gone.

A flash of lightning outside the windows highlights the vampiress as she studies a large hole in the wall that once housed the staircase leading down to the secret chamber. Diana cautiously stands next to the senior officer and studies the set of three stairs that lead to nothing more than a pile of rubble. Deloris descends the three steps to study the stone, muttering a few unkind words as she punches the impassible object.

Whoever destroyed the stairs have made sure it was truly solid and impassable. It is also likely that the chamber the stairs lead to is also destroyed. Artemis studies the wall then turns around suddenly, weapon in hand. Diana also whips around to see nothing is there, at least right now. Deloris, seeing the actions of her companions, casually turns around to face the room.

"Why did you return?" Agatha asks as she appears in a flash, combining with the lightning outside. "Are you here to bring news of my sister's passing?"

"We do not know if Theresa has passed or not, last we saw she was alive in prison," Deloris answers. "Why do you ask?"

"Because I am waiting for her," Agatha admits. "Awaiting so that we both can travel to the spirit world together."

"You were once a Captor for the Cult of Amamet," Diana says. "Do you happen to know where they would have hidden the statue of Amamet?"

"Both of you have seen the mural on the wall that comes from Amamet's tomb," Agatha says with a ghostly grin. "The answer is drawn there and perhaps you missed the clue as you focused on the characters. Perhaps you need to think about the objects in the mural as well."

"Objects?" Diana frowns.

"Each object and indeed person in the mural can have a single meaning or dual meanings," the ghost continues. "Your answer, dear child, is written on the wall...."

"Did the Egyptologist miss that in her interpretation?" Deloris questions.

"It is very likely that she was focused on the past and not the present," Agatha says. "Perhaps, when you think of the objects, you will figure out what represents a more modern symbol. You are very close, though. Yes, close indeed."

The storm outside slows down to a whimper as the sunlight breaks the clouds apart. Agatha smiles at those in front of her before she seems to melt into the sun rays streaming in the window. Diana grumbles about riddles as she turns and leads the way out of the room and back into the main area of the Expo Building. They pause upon reaching the main room and peer into the darkness once again.

With the new light, they can see a strange stage that is at least twenty feet above the main floor halfway into the building itself. Beyond a few rails is a darker shadow as if something is purposefully keeping itself hidden. Deloris focuses on the shadows and arches an eyebrow when she hears the faint whisper of someone breathing. The doors suddenly burst open as several security bots come into the building each with their lights flashing. Deloris scowls at the mechanical beings as they demand that the intruders leave the building immediately.

Instead of fighting or arguing, the trio decides to quietly obey the orders and slowly walk to the open doors. The robots herd the uninvited guests until they leave the building then close the doors, locking them tightly. Deloris turns to look at the doors of the building as she contemplates the strange behavior of the robots. A chime goes off on Diana's phone orb prompting her to take it out of her pocket and glance at the message.

"It looks like Uncle Julius's meeting was short," Diana notices. "I have to find someplace where I can call him back."

"Does the library have private rooms?" Deloris inquires.

"I had not noticed the first time I went there but it is worth a look," Diana admits.

The library doors whine open allowing Diana and Deloris to enter. Per usual students are filling every available seat in the main room. To save time, the two officers decide to split up to look for a private room they can commandeer for the phone call. Instead of heading to the museum part of the library, Diana circles around the outer edges of the bookcases until she finds a room. Unfortunately, it is currently occupied by a sleeping L'phant. The large hulking alien being fills up half the space of the small room with its tail blocking the door.

Deloris catches up with Diana and her Aethoes to inform them that this room is the only private room in the library. Diana carefully weighs her options before she politely knocks on the door to the room. Through the glass, they watch as the L'phant opens his eyes and turns to the door casually lifting his tail to allow it to open a crack.

"Excuse me," Diana addresses the occupant.

"What do you want, puny human?" the L'phant snaps, his brooding voice full of disdain.

"I need to use this room for a business matter," Diana says frankly.

"Did you see me sleeping, human?" the L'phant once again snaps unapologetically.

"You are an intergalactic student of this university. Thus, you have a dorm room on campus," Diana points out. "You can catch your nap in your room."

"You are a bold, puny, human to tell me where I can or cannot sleep," the L'phant laughs harshly. "I do as I please, puny human, even as far as murdering you without consequences. Now go away before I enact my rights."

The L'phant flexes his tail and slams the door shut. Diana takes a deep breath in and slowly releases it as she places a hand upon the door. She hesitates and turns to her Aethoes when Artemis touches her on the shoulder. Diana simply nods and moves out of the way to stand next to Deloris. Both P.I.U. officers watch the inside of the room as Artemis grabs the door handle and turns it.

The occupant of the room snorts and once again flexes his tail only for the door to pushback and slams his tail into the wall pinning it between the two obstacles. The L'phant bellows in rage as he turns to face the intruder with his eyes lit up like coal. Artemis silently motions that the beast should remain quiet which only enrages him further. He lunges towards his prey only for his fist to connect with something solid and unyielding. The sudden stop of his motion jars his entire body, harshly.

Artemis captures the L'phant's wrist and casually tosses him out of the room. He tumbles until he slams into one of the free-standing bookcases. The fragile wooden structure collapses and buries him under a mountain of manuscripts. Artemis then motions for Deloris and Diana to come into the room as the L'phant frees himself with another bellow of rage. He charges as the two P.I.U. officers crossed the threshold of the room. Artemis glares at the charging creature and casually slams the door shut.

The L'phant rams into the door but it does not shatter from his weight or his charge. He bangs upon it angrily alerting the mechanical library staff of trouble near the conference room. A group of security bots rush over and seize the offending student. He roars and kicks as he is dragged out of the library and banned from it for the rest of the school year.

"That ended rather well," Deloris admits. "It also appears that Artemis has gained a few new abilities since the link was reestablished."

"L'phants are stubborn and very rude inherently," Diana informs. "If he had broken through the door, I think he might have lost his life."

"I can see that," Deloris agrees. "You need to contact Julius now. Did you want me to leave to give you some privacy?"

"I think it is a better strategy that you stay since Uncle Julius likes you," Diana assures. "Your presence should lessen the blow I'm about to receive."

"La dispozitia ta," Deloris says with a little smile.

Diana places her phone orb on the table and casually spends it. The rotating device starts to levitate off the table as it dials. A holographic image of a stern-looking man is replaced by a miniature replica of him sitting at a desk. Diana grins at her uncle and greets him casually even as he brings up the two documents that they are to discuss. He does not say a word as the young woman clarifies to him what happened to warrant the two documents. Julius continues to stare at his niece as if he is mulling over the explanation.

"Tsk, Julius. Diana has had a very rough week," Deloris scolds mildly. "You can forgive the girl for being just a little short-tempered with those that provide false accusations."

"Who is that?" Julius inquires slowly.

"Awe, Julius. Don't tell me we were apart for so long you forgot me," Deloris teases as she scoots closer to the intern in order to get into the view of the phone orb's camera.

"Deloris," Julius smiles, his eyes lighting up with glee. "I've not seen you since Diana joined the force. How are you?"

"I'm well. How are you doing, handsome?" Deloris retorts. Diana quietly breathes as she prepares to take over the conversation.

"I am miles better since I see you, beautiful," Julius flirts. He shakes his head as if sobering up. "Wait, why are you with Diana at Morstone University?"

"We are in an ongoing investigation, Uncle," Diana informs. "Twin investigations actually. But I think you want to focus on the letter sent by Dr. Pikeys."

"Ah yes, first. How was your week? Melody tells me that it was a bit rocky," Julius leans forward once again and focuses on his niece. "Do you want to talk about it?"

"Diana has reconnected with her Aethoes," Deloris explains instead. "They are still learning each other's abilities and what they can achieve together. It will take a little time."

"I see, very well we can talk later about it," Julius relents. "This letter tells me that you cheated on a test and are facing expulsion."

"I did not cheat on the test, uncle," Diana starts but quiets when the man raises his hand slightly.

"I know this. I took a look at the question and compared it to the knowledge that you would gain from your internship. Especially since you are mentored by Deloris," Julius continues his thoughts. "Thus, I will be sending Dr. Pikeys a long and strongly worded letter about these accusations and the fact that I am pulling you out of this college and canceling my sponsorship of it."

"Ouch, that's going to hurt their bottom-line," Diana flinches a little as if she received a slight blow.

"However, I still want you to have a deeper understanding of your chosen field," Julius informs his niece. "Deloris, you are as lovely as you are deadly, but I believe Diana needs a more in-depth education than what you are able to provide."

"I agree," Deloris nods. "I have a few suggestions if you'd like to hear them."

"I would love to talk to you about them, however, I have already made arrangements with Dracorn University in the Aligon Territory," Julius announces. "Diana, you will be in residence on the campus. You will meet your sponsor when she has time."

"Wait, Aligon Territory?" Diana shakes her head as she processes the information. "Uncle, that's going to take a little while to prepare for. First I need a passport..."

"All paperwork and preparations have been done," Julius informs. "All you have to do is show up to the campus in two weeks."

"Ok, Uncle. But how will I get there?" Diana questions. The Aligon Territory is clearly on the other side of the planet."

"Not as bad as the other side of the galaxy," Julius says with a mischievous grin. "I have made arrangements for your transportation. You will get there in time to get familiar with the campus and your accommodations. I will go with you for the first day then you will be on your own."

"I am surprised at the speed at which you achieved that is amazing, Julius," Deloris points out. "Getting into the Dracorn is not easy."

"I have many amazing qualities about me, Deloris," Julius says, huskily.

"I'm sure," Deloris retorts.

"Diana, I missed your visit this week but understand why. Will I see you tomorrow?" Julius asks. "I need to talk to you about the link you have to your Aethos as well as the new college you will be attending."

"I will see if I can get the day off, Uncle," Diana assures. "However, I would like to finish this investigation first."

"Ah yes, you did say you were in the middle of the investigation. I will let you finish with your case," Julius says. "Deloris. Ne vedem mai tarziu." The phone orb goes silent and slowly lowers back down to the table.

"Your uncle is a flirt," Deloris informs. "For a minute I did not know if my mind control abilities accidentally activated and were working on him or if he had control over me."

"I am still stunned about Dracorn," Diana admits. "I'm tempted to go to his house now to sit down and talk to him. But I know if I leave, especially with Uncle Julius's return letter to Pikeys, I will not be able to come back on campus."

"You will be able to return, on official P.I.U. business," Deloris assures. "However, we are here now and it takes a while to get back to H.Q. Especially during traffic. So, we might as well wait until the supposed tribute for the victims to see what really happens."

Diana watches students walking past the window of the conference room as Deloris dials Lawson's number. It rings several times before going to voicemail. Deloris leaves a message for the commissioner then hangs up and turns to the intern. A knock comes to the door and Diana carefully answers it. It is the library staff politely requesting that they leave the building. Diana is an unauthorized student within the facilities. Deloris informs the staff that they are in the middle of an investigation. The staff does not budge on their orders and also informs Deloris that she is banned as well from the campus. Once both women leave, they will not be able to return without the security bots arresting them.

Diana frowns at the information as she peacefully leaves the building, walking beside her Aethoes. Deloris lingers a little longer then follows after the intern. The doors to the library close behind them, leaving them outside and among the crowd of students rushing to classes. Diana finds a bench under a tree to camp out on and sits back to relax and observe the environment.

"So now we wait until sunset," Deloris muses as she sits down then leans back on the bench.

The sun finally gives way to nightfall as the super full moon rises to illuminate the campus. The haunting light is enough for the last stragglers of the day to find their way to their car unaided by the streetlights. Those that dwell on campus head to their dorms which intrigues both Diana and Deloris. Apparently, no one knows about the memorial that is only moments away from kicking off.

Artemis's bright golden glow catches Diana's attention and causes Deloris to put her sunglasses back on. The brightness of the light is a little discomforting to the vampiress's eyes. The door to the Expo building opens up to an unexpected event. Artemis tones her glow down as several hooded men walked out of the building chanting in an ancient dialect. They are also burning strange incense and carrying a strange-looking vessel upon their shoulder. The hooded caravan makes its way to the front door of the fraternity house, going methodically through the door. The chant continues to stir for several more minutes and then stops.

"What were they chanting?" Diana inquires.

"Something far more dangerous than the spell I used earlier," Deloris frowns. "A few of them are chanting Soul Eater in repetition."

"Seriously? Do they have another victim in there?" Diana stares into the doorway of the fraternity house. "Do we go in?"

"Or do we go into the Expo building?" Deloris counters.

The officers go quiet when they see a few more people leave the Expo building and head into the fraternity house. Diana recognizes one of the people as Laurie dressed in one of the strange hooded robes. It is similar to the one used by those who stole Amamet's statue from the museum according to the video footage. Those with her continue to hide their features as they follow her into the doorway.

The candlelight that they use to see their way fills the interior briefly and then fades. Diana carefully approaches the front door of the fraternity house and peeks in even as her senses warn her of danger in the air. Deloris stands on the opposite side of the door and removes her shades to peer into the darkness of the interior. The air from the inside is ripe with both fear and blood.

This information causes the senior officer to mutter under her breath as she shakes her head.

Diana backs off and goes over towards the Expo building to try the doors finding them lock tight. She returns and informs her companions of the discovery. Artemis frowns at the news and unshoulders her bow to notch an arrow. She increases the glow about her once again and carefully enters into the darkness. The golden light barely penetrates the void yet nothing dangerous presents itself. Diana follows her Aethoes into the frat house next and is flanked by Deloris. The foyer is empty much like the Expo building. All of the furniture is gone to include the chandelier. It is replaced by strange hieroglyphics upon the wall and wide-eyed women painted on the ceiling.

As they take in the strange scene, the door behind them slams shut triggering all to turn around quickly. Her instincts scream causing Diana to turn back to the room, cuss, and then jump out of the way. Deloris is not as quick to avoid the light whip as it wraps around her and gives her a mighty shock, dropping her immediately. Diana swears again and scrambles to assist Deloris as Artemis takes aim in the direction the whip came from and fires.

The arrow disappears briefly before returning at full speed aimed at the archer. Artemis dodges to one side and catches the arrow as Diana reaches for the unconscious Deloris. The intern expresses surprise once again when the vampiress disappears down a very deep dark hole that opens up underneath her. The floor under Diana starts to move prompting the young lady to swiftly get off of it and onto solid ground. Diana repeats the exercise several times to avoid the pitfalls. Artemis moves to assist her mortal doppelgänger but instead moves out of the way as the light whip returns and barely misses her.

A duplicate of the arrow she launched earlier nearly skewers Artemis yet she avoids it with only a scratch. Diana sees the arrow coming and dodges it which unfortunately causes her to fall down one of the pit traps that she had successfully avoided until now. Artemis sees Diana go down and cusses as she dodges both whip and arrow, notching her own ammunition and aims at the door. She lets one arrow fly, as the bolt connects with the door it explodes sending smoke and debris into the air.

Artemis quickly exits the house and rolls out of range of the whip. She stands up facing the house to see that the door has reformed itself and is now locked tight. Artemis also discovers that the link with Diana is weak or temporally disconnected as the young woman did not respond when called out to. A deep scowl knits her brow as she sets her sights on the far tower of the fraternity house and makes her way toward it.

CHAPTER TEN

The Reveal

A piercing light flashes across her closed eyes. She swears in her native tongue as she turns over. The cold of a stone floor chills her cheek as she gathers her wits about her. The droning of heavy voices finally breaks through the forced sleep imposed upon the senior P.I.U. officer. A threatening sound emits from Deloris as she slowly pulls her arms closer to her form. Her fingers dig into the stone briefly during the trip ending with her pushing up into a sitting position.

Deloris shakes her head to try and clear her sight, it is still fuzzy from the electric attack that dropped her. She plants one foot on the ground and uses her knee as leverage to stand up. Her ailments disappear as she takes in the situation she has awakened to. She is now in a strangely lit cage and is surrounded by a great number of kneeling worshipers each with their back to her.

Deloris directs her attention to the item that the cult members are bowing towards. Deloris whispers unkind words when she sees the enormous statue of Amamet mounted on the platform twenty feet off the ground. In front of the statue are two columns covered in hieroglyphics, topped with red and orange flames flickering above. Connected to the columns are two long and heavy ropes. In the center of the pillars as well as connected to the rope is a secondary cage and an unconscious Diana.

The sight stuns Deloris as she walks over to the bars of her cage and grabs them. She receives a strong shock that breaks her grip on the bars and sends her back a couple of feet. Deloris takes in any damage done to her hands then looks up quickly when a whip made of light slaps the bars creating additional sparks.

"Not so haughty now, are you bitch?" Raine Pikeys gloats to her captive.

"I'm not the one wearing the collar," Deloris says as she quickly scans the perpetrator.

"That can be arranged," Raine chuckles as she slaps the bars with her whip again.

"Even if you attempt to place that offending apparatus upon my neck, you will be eating it as I stuff it down your throat before I rip it out," Deloris informs, bluntly.

"There are so many urban legends surrounding you, Deloris. Yet you are so easily captured," Raine boasts and cracks her whip again. "I expected a little bit more out of you."

"Once I get past these bars, I will show you how true those supposed legends are," Deloris promises.

"Oh, really now," Raine grins as she approaches the cage and stares directly into Deloris's eyes. "I will have your head before you cross the distance."

"Open the cage," Deloris demands.

"You will have to do better than that," Raine laughs at her captive.

Deloris sneers at her challenger as Raine turns her back to the bars. The senior officer carefully studies the cage bars. She deciphers that there is some sort of mystical means that dampens her abilities built into the structure. The irritating droning stops as a small procession of people enter the room. Deloris looks up at the new arrivals to see that there are three men and a woman dressed as if they are part of the mural at the museum.

One of the men, as the high priest, to no surprise, is Beryl. A second man has attire similarly to Dr. Pikeys with a spiked collar and leather straps upon his body. The textile barely hides his manhood. The third and final man flanking the woman has a bowl full of dark red liquid and is the high priest's assistant.

The High Priestess of Amamet is dressed in only the finest fabric. A golden crown circles her brow, accenting her waves of lush blonde hair. The barely dressed man approaches Deloris's cage and grins at her, revealing that he too is a vampire. Deloris meets his gaze and simply glares into his eyes, quickly connecting to his subconscious mind.

The man's grin starts to fade when he finds that he cannot break away from the battle of the minds. Raine lets out an angry sound as she slaps the cage with her whip. The sound and action break the trance, aiding the male vampire to look away. Deloris calmly turns her gaze back to Raine and does not flinch when the whip strikes again.

"So, this is the infamous Deloris Matox," the high priestess says as she approaches the cage. "I've heard many stories about you. It seems that you do disappoint in person. You may be marginally stronger than Raine but apparently not as clever."

"I will assure you, Laurie, that there is nothing clever about Raine," Deloris informs calmly. "She just happened to get a lucky strike at that time. As soon as I get out of this cage, I will be snapping her neck and sending her straight to the underworld."

"You will be making the trip more so than I," Raine snarls in response.

"You have no idea, girl, whom you are trifling with," Deloris warns steadily.

"I like this animosity," Laurie grins happily. "The entertainment it promises after this special sacrifice will be well worth the wait."

"There was a second mystic among you when you stole the statue of Amamet," Deloris recalls. "Is she here as well? If so then your entertainment is only beginning."

"It is sad and unfortunate that her highness could not be here," Laurie responds confidently. "She did, however, provide the instruments for your capture. She also gave me strict instructions on how to properly sacrifice Diana."

"You will be a fool if you carry this out," Deloris warns.

"Says the one in the cage," Laurie laughs and walks away.

Deloris watches Laurie walks away and converse with Beryl about the night's plans. She ignores Raine when the whip strikes the bars yet again. The senior officer turns her attention back to the raised floor as she notices that Diana has yet to awaken from slumber. Laurie traverses up the ramp and stands directly in front of the cage that her victim is safely tucked behind for now.

A strange noise from Wyliam brings Deloris's attention briefly back to him as she sees that the male vampire is dangerously focused upon the cage with the unconscious young woman. The smell of fresh blood slaps Deloris in the face and directs her senses to the stranger carrying the bowl of liquid. He approaches the cage that holds Diana and grins maliciously at the cantankerous former student. Laurie turns and faces the crowd of worshipers.

"Tonight is the night that we will take back our rightful place among the immortals," Laurie announces with great enthusiasm. "We will revive Amamet and with her under my command shall crush all naysayers and force compliance from the masses."

"Oh, great and powerful priestess," the man with the bowl addresses quietly. "What about the link that her highness warned us about?"

"I am well aware of the link, Mr. Murphy, and if she shows up, she too will be sacrificed," Laurie assures just as quietly. She once again focuses on her audience. "Open the roof then lower the victim's cage."

A terrible shriek puts Deloris's teeth on edge as metal scrapes against itself and the deep rumbling of heavy-duty motors fill the room. The wind speed inside the space starts to pick up as the Expo dome splits with the two halves folding down to reveal the sky. The bright light of the super full hunter's moon illuminates the entire room.

The elevated floor shakes slightly as the cage around Diana sinks into the floor. The young woman groans a little as she tries to wake up yet something keeps her under. Mr. Murphy lifts his bowl of blood provoking a sound of glee to echo in the room from various worshipers. The droning resumes led by Beryl as he lifts a strange dark orb.

"Diana, get up!" Artemis scolds in the young woman's mind. "GET UP!"

Diana jerks her head up quickly and comes to her feet before she is even fully awake. Her balance is slightly off as she stumbles a little then clears her head and takes in her surroundings. The chanting worshipers are the first thing she notices with the sure number in various sizes of them. Her eyesight fuzzes up a little as she reaches to hold her head only for her arm to stop halfway there.

Alert now she stares at the rope that is binding her and follows it to see that it is connected to the large columns as well. She turns to the other side to see that she is bound on both arms and legs with very little room for escape. Diana swears as she sees Prof. Murphy holding up a strange bowl of red liquid, she presumes is blood, and Beryl opposite of Laurie lifting the orb. All three currently have their backs to her. Diana scans around the room, locating Deloris inside of the cage on the lower level. The senior officer is guarded by Dr. Pikeys and Laurie's supposed fiancé, Wyliam. The hair on the back of Diana's neck rises as she carefully glances over her shoulder. The missing statue of Amamet grins at her mockingly.

"Oh, hell…. What is this…" Diana stutters finding it a little hard to formulate her thoughts at the moment. "Wait, this is the Expo building. The frat house."

"Ah, finally awake I see," Laurie observes as she turns to face her latest victim.

"Awake and very un-humored," Diana assures.

"You will be fine in a matter of a few minutes," Laurie beams. "I will give you this, you were a hard target to catch. It took a little innovation to actually get you off guard."

"Innovation meaning that you nearly killed Raquel after her attempts to lure me to your 'parties'," Diana says, anger trickling in her words. "Why did you target me?"

"Because, little girl, you have a connection that her highness finds very offensive yet entirely useful in the revival of our sect," Laurie explains as she approaches her victim and stands only a few inches away. "Any other questions before you die?"

"The security camera at the Museum of Past Modern History shows that there was an accomplice in the removal of Amamet's statue. She appears to have stronger metaphysical abilities than you," Diana points out calmly. "Where is she?"

"Your annoying attitude will soon be a memory," Laurie snorts in distaste of the observation. "Her highness is not here for this sacrifice as she claims to have other business to take care of. However, if your twin shows up, perhaps we can persuade her to return for a very special night."

The high priestess walks away from her victim as the moonlight illuminates the entire area. Diana feels it wash over her body and an increase in mystical strength from the lunar rays. She looks over to see Beryl lift a dark orb above his head and it gently lifts off his hand to levitate several feet above him. The excitement in the room heightens as Laurie approaches Amamet then points to the orb. It pulsates once before those who were sacrificed scream or yowl as they exit the container and swirl around the room. They spiral quickly, spinning within the confines of an invisible ceiling and unable to escape into the night.

Diana closes her eyes to blot out the noises of the lost souls as she focuses on locating her Aethoes. A deep, guttural sound exits the statue as it very slightly opens its mouth. The noise breaks Diana's concentration as she glances back at the beast to see the eyes flash slightly. She swears bitterly as she tries to pull on her bonds. Out of the corner of her eyes, Diana sees Prof. Murphy approach her with the bowl of blood. A strange hiss and growl sound to her left catches her attention.

Diana turns to observe Wyliam fixate upon her as he stalks closer to her. Several of the captured souls swirl around the chained woman and then are directed straight into Amamet's mouth. Diana swears again, feeling a strong boost of energy as the light of the full moon brightens considerably. She pauses in her words and activity when she hears a familiar voice echo inside her mind.

"Stop struggling, Ms. Hunter," Prof. Murphy says with glee. "I did warn you at the start of the week that if you did not change your attitude you would end up in a peculiar situation."

"I remember your words Mr. Murphy," Diana acknowledges. "It will behoove you not to go through with this ceremony, professor. You are already looking at being an accomplice to several murders."

"You have no power in your situation, Ms. Hunter," Murphy snorts. "Your idle threats mean nothing here."

"As I alluded to earlier, I do not make idle threats or promises," Diana reiterates.

Two arrows whistle through the air and slice the ropes holding Diana in place. Murphy shouts obscenities as he tosses the blood at the young woman. Diana holds up her hand, freezing the liquid in place then reversing its course to splash upon Murphy. The man's angry words are replaced with a cry of terror as he turns and faces Wyliam. The male vampire is only inches from him yet appears to be in a trance and does not attack.

Diana finishes freeing herself of the ropes and looks up to see Artemis standing upon the side of the open dome. The Aethoes takes aim at the cage holding Deloris and fires off two additional arrows. The bolts sing briefly as one slam into the lock, destroying the gate of the cage and the other barely misses Raine as she dodges out of the way. Deloris's eyes turn blood orange briefly as a deadly grin comes to her features. She carefully exits the cage and takes in the view of the entire area.

"That was close, wasn't it, Raine?" Deloris says and smiles when her challenger turns around.

"Wyliam, come to me," Raine commands. She frowns when there is no response. "Wyliam."

"Do you mean the male?" Deloris inquires with a slight nod of her head in the direction of the subject.

Raine glances over her shoulder to see that her underling is still frozen in place. Deloris simply raises her hand and snaps her fingers. Wyliam collapses to the ground, unconscious. Raine is stunned at first and then angered as she rapidly turns back to her opponent and uses her weapon, aiming at Deloris's throat. The whip goes through Deloris as the senior officer disappears into a mist.

Raine recoils her whip as the mist surrounds her and Deloris reforms to knock the weapon out of the woman's hand and her own hand goes around Raine's throat. Deloris's grip upon her opponent is quickly loosened as the woman drops to the ground in a pile of black scorpions. Deloris curses and quickly dodges out of the way of the angry swarm, taking care to retrieve the light-whip in her haste. The scorpions crawl a short distance away before coalescing into Raine. Deloris focuses on Raine as she holds up the whip and crushes the base, destroying the weapon. Raine hisses in anger as she lunges forward to attack Deloris.

An arrow slams into the floor in front of Laurie, breaking her concentration. The captured souls suddenly reverse and start to spin about the room searching for an exit. Artemis reloads her bow as Laurie faces her. Thunder is heard briefly before a bolt crash into the archer resulting in an abundance of unkind words from her.

Artemis gathers the remaining energy from the lightning and sends it directly to Laurie. The high priestess catches the lightning and slides backward for several feet, slamming into one of the columns before she could dispel it. Diana dodges out of the way of the collapsing column, barely avoiding the large slabs of marble. Prof. Murphy turns in time for the slab to fall onto him, knocking him to the ground. He has no time to cry out as the debris buries him completely. Wyliam is also buried and does not react as he is still unconscious. Artemis quickly takes aim at the second column and destroys it's base, sending the go-liath in the direction of the high priestess.

Laurie shrieks in surprise as the column comes down quickly to bury her in a pile of rubble and pebbles. Diana stands from her hasty retreat and glances up to her Aethoes. A burning sensation next to her skin catches her by surprise. Diana quickly locates the source of the pain is not her awakened abilities but an item in her jacket pocket. She reaches in and pulls out the coin of Isis.

An instant later, Diana dodges left then leaps back as she avoids Beryl as he tries to stab her with the Dagger of Anubis. Beryl sneers as he unleashes a flash of light heading towards the intern. Diana is caught off guard and slapped by the spell, acci-dentally dropping the coin of Isis at the same time. She turns to try and retrieve it as it rolls away only to move away when Beryl once again swipes at her with the dagger.

Diana straightens up and moves to one side as he takes an-other stab at her. She grabs his wrist and twists it harshly, causing him to drop the dagger. Diana kicks the dagger out of the way and twists Beryl's arm again. The man hollers and falls to his knees as pain racks his body. Several fraternity brothers rush forward only to stop in their tracks as an explosion blocks the way. Artemis lands on the floor and picks up the coin of Isis. The coin pulsates in her hand and the souls begin to reverse, go-ing back into the orb.

"You are livelier than the last two ladies," Beryl says through gritted teeth.

"I suggest that you adhere to your right to remain silent," Diana said.

"Oh really, I will have to resist arrest then," Beryl assures.

Diana stumbles forward slightly as Beryl disappears. She quickly looks up and turns when he appears next to the discarded Dagger of Anubis. Beryl picks up the weapon and tosses it, aiming directly at Diana. She takes a step back then jumps, allowing the dagger to sail underneath her. Diana lands next to her Aethoes as the Dagger of Anubis clatters harmlessly to the floor several feet behind her. Beryl lights up suddenly then sends a wave of green light towards his intended victim.

Artemis shifts her bow to her opposite hand then does a quick motion with her free hand. The green web curves back on itself as it careens back to its originator. Beryl is caught off guard at the reversal of his incantation and yelps in pain as it slams back into him. The frat leader's body suddenly freezes in place then falls over. The rest of the fraternity brothers gather their courage and charge forward. Diana prepares to charge then hesitates when her Aethoes places her arm in front to stop her. Artemis then does a short whistle. Several hounds leap out of thin air and charge towards the approaching frat brothers. The group quickly stops the charge and reverses course as they run from the dogs.

With a pack of snapping dogs at their heels, the fraternity brother mass exit from the building. A few of them try to battle with the canines only to succumb and flee with the rest of their brothers. Deloris notices the brother's exiting the building but kept her current opponent. She takes a step back and catches Raine when she jumps at her then tosses the woman into a group of retreating frat brothers.

Raine lets out a vicious sound as she grabs one of the brothers she landed on and sinks her teeth into his neck. The young man yells once before he dies. Deloris shakes her head then sidesteps the body that Raine pitches at her. The senior officer recovers quickly and catches her opponent in midair. In one swift movement, Deloris slams Raine onto the ground and holds her there. The superintendent tries to transform but finds that she cannot do so. She then tries to push up off the ground but feels a heavy weight settle upon her back. Deloris continues to apply pressure as she steps down on the back of Raine's neck to keep her in place.

"You have made several mistakes Raine Pikeys," Deloris says.

"Get off, bitch," Raine snarls.

"No need to get testy," Deloris retorts and leans forward. "I will ask for leniency for you only if you tell me where I can find Medea."

"I will never betray Her Highness," Raine says defiantly. "I would rather face death then her wrath."

"Loyalty to her is not worth your life. Do not be foolish," Deloris reasons.

"You do not know what she is capable of," Raine says.

"I am fully aware of her capabilities. We are blood," Deloris admits.

"What?" Raine's eyes widened from the statement.

"Diana time to wrap this case up," Deloris calls up to the platform.

"Yes ma'am," Diana calls back.

The souls still being returned to the orb yowl softly as they are sucked back into the prison. The cloud of spirits is now smaller as everything is cleared out. Diana casually approaches the statue of Amamet to study the item so that she can come up with a plan to return it to the museum. Artemis lackadaisically flips the Coin of Isis, catching it in mid-air.

The pile of rubble that buried Laurie moves slightly catching the Aethoes's attention immediately. Diana pauses when she hears a warning from Artemis about the pile. The intern turns quickly then jumps up and back when the pile of rubble explodes as the High Priestess frees herself. The souls stop their slow reversal and quickly start going back into Amamet's mouth as flames light up around Laurie. Diana lands at the very edge of the platform, quickly taking a couple of steps forward so that she would not fall over.

"This is not over!" Laurie yells angrily as a strong wave of pressure spreads out quickly from her being.

The wave hits Artemis first then slams into Diana, sending the young woman over the edge. The intern swears and quickly twists to catch the ledge, preventing a twenty-foot drop. Diana pulls herself back onto the platform as the rubble around Laurie lifts and circulates rapidly. Artemis scowls as Laurie sends several large boulders towards her. She dodges one, splits a second in half and obliterates a third.

Sand and dust fill the air from the destruction. Diana takes advantage of Laurie's distraction and charges forward, dodging through the field of floating rocks, and shouldering the high priestess to send her to the ground. Laurie turns over and glares at the woman that knocked her down.

Diana goes to pin the high priestess down when a sound from the statue distracts her. The intern turns to see Amamet's eyes flash again as the mouth opens just a little wider. An invisible force grabs Diana and lifts her involuntarily into the air. A boulder also rises as Laurie once again stands up. The high priestess yells as she first sends the large boulder towards Artemis then follows it with the intern. Diana cries out in surprise as she sails back towards her Aethoes.

Artemis destroys the boulder in a rain of dust and takes aim at the second item heading towards her. She swears and lowers her weapon in time to be impacted by Diana. Both hit the ground, harshly. Laurie expresses her satisfaction as she pulls the orb back in place and the flow of souls increases to an alarming rate. The statue moans in response to the influx.

"Laurie is a powerful bugger and Amamet is about to roar back to life," Diana observes then turns to her Aethoes. "What's the plan?"

The glow around Artemis brightens considerably as she glares at Laurie and Amamet. The Aethoes then turns to her mortal doppelgänger and simply holds up her hand. Diana is confused at first and then bravely takes the offered appendage.

The immediate surge of power makes the young woman nearly fall to her knees from the pain it creates. Laurie yells in anger as she sends a bolt of energy towards the two. It slams into a powerful arcane shield and mixes with the brightening illumination. The light suddenly peaks in brightness, blinding all in the room and robbing Deloris of her concentration which allows Raine to break free. The superintendent runs out of the room and is followed hotly by her opponent.

It does not take very long for Raine to reach the front door and dive through it only to hit the ground once again as Deloris tackles her. The two tussle for several moments until a bullet strikes the ground right next to them. Deloris is first to look up and pause in her actions when she sees Lawson casually put his gun back in its holster.

The senior P.I.U. officer scans around the area to see that they are surrounded by the Middle District Police Department and arrested members of the Alpha Norma Sigma fraternity. Deloris carefully stands up, mindful to keep a foot on Raine as the P.I.U. commissioner approaches.

"I got your message," Lawson admits. "Safe to say you did not get mine."

"No," Deloris says. "I was a little busy apprehending a suspect."

"Looks like you were beating the hell out of her," Lawson acknowledges with a grin. "And you look like she was returning the favor."

"It appears that way. I was captured and caged but it's a long story," Deloris explains.

"Can't wait to hear it. So, where's the intern?" Lawson inquires.

"Diana and her Aethoes are currently engaged in apprehending the ringleader of this circus," Deloris explains.

The glow in the room starts to fade as the souls stop in midstream and once again reverse back into the orb this time at an increased rate. Those that are undigested exit Amamet and also return to the dark globe. Artemis studies her mortal doppelgänger to see that her breathing has actually changed. Diana looks up and slowly gets back to her feet as she nods to her Aethoes, assuring that she is fine. Laurie whispers a few profanities as Diana faces her once again.

A golden glint just beyond her opponent catches her eye as she recognizes the Dagger of Anubis. Diana is about to once again charge when she hears the scraping of the golden dagger just behind her. The young woman turns in time for both she and her Aethoes to quickly dodge the item as Laurie calls it to her hand. The dagger slows and presents the handle to the high priestess as she sneers at those in front of her.

"Amamet, I willingly give you my soul so that you can terminate the ones that desecrated you," Laurie announces and lifts the dagger above her head, glaring at her audience. "My death will be the beginning of your destruction."

"Laurie wait," Diana calls.

The Dagger of Anubis hums as Laurie brings it down to pierce her own stomach. Her eyes widened as the dagger slips from her hand and falls to the ground. There is no blood on the weapon or flowing from her wound, instead, a dark substance bellows out like smoke from her stomach. Her eyes turn blank as her body crumbles to the floor. The soul of Laurie coagulates into a ghostly form of the woman and sneers once again at the audience.

The soul then quickly slips directly into Amamet's mouth. The platform starts to vibrate angrily prompting swears from both Diana and Artemis as they hop off of it into the main floor. The statue's eyes flash to life, glowing menacingly as the mouth snaps shut and the head twists from side to side. Amamet shakes

off the stone casting and roars as she turns in search of her op-
ponents.

Artemis motions for Diana to stay silent as she gently informs her mortal doppelgänger that the fantastic beast is not yet
at full strength. Diana quietly relaxes as the news brings a little
relief as she whispers her question of a course of action. Artemis
explains how she and Pakheth defeated Amamet before and lets
Diana know that the impending battle is still going to be very intense despite the beast's handicap.

"Seriously," Diana reacts to the news louder than she intends.

The entire dome trembles as Amamet roars loudly and
jumps from the platform to land on the main floor. Artemis gives
Diana a scolding look before the two dodge the snapping jaws of
the creature. Amamet goes after Artemis first intentionally
swishing the crocodilian head in order to knock her down.

Artemis avoids the maul, parries, and fires a single shot
into the mouth of her attacker. To her dismay, there is no effect
from the single shot. She quickly jumps as Amamet lunges at her
and knocks down the wall that once led to Ms. Cummins's classroom. Artemis lands on the platform once again and quickly
scans the area in search of Diana. She finds her dodging the tail
of the monster and somehow managing to end up on the beast's
backend. Diana takes in her situation and holds on as Amamet
stomps around the area in search of her. The young woman immediately thinks about having a knife of some sort and is
surprised when the weapon appears in her hand. Diana stares at
the item for several seconds and then shrugs it off.

"So much for 'taking it slow'," Diana remarks right before she stabs the rump of Amamet.

Artemis's laughter is barely heard above Amamet's roar of pain and surprise. Diana holds on as the beast bucks and turns to cause massive destruction to the Expo building's floor. The platform twists and turns from the earthquake-like vibrations, yet remain in place. Diana sees her opportunity and jumps from the beast's back and barely avoids the teeth of the crocodile head as she lands on the platform next to her Aethoes.

The intern gains her balance and her senses as she conjures up a bow in one hand and arrow in the next. She and Artemis then aim at the beast. Diana adjusts her aim a little when she is instructed to do so. Before they could release their arrows, however, Amamet uses her offended rump and slams it against the platform. The action causes both archers to misfire as they lose their balance yet they remain upon the platform. Both hold on as their perch is shaken once again by the agitated beast.

Diana rolls into a kneeling position as Artemis gets to her feet. The dual draw back their bows as three arrows apiece appear upon the string. Amamet rears up with jaws agape and claws extended, a red flame is seen within the depths of her mouth. Artemis aims at the chest of the monster and releases her bolts and is followed closely by Diana. All six arrows hit their mark and Amamet bellows in pain as she falls backward. She returns to a stone statue and hit the concrete floor, shattering into a pile of pebbles from the impact. Diana's bow disappears as she carefully places her hands upon the ground as well as her second knee. She pants as she tries to rein in her rapid breathing, feeling the strain of the ordeal she just endured.

"I'm all right," Diana assures when Artemis touches her back. "I just need a minute to understand what just happened."

Diana carefully stands up and steadies her balance by leaning against her Aethoes briefly. The discarded dark orb of souls shimmies in the moonlight and beckons the young woman towards it. Diana picks up the orb and the Dagger of Anubis being careful to wrap both in Laurie's discarded robe. Artemis jumps from the platform to the main floor avoiding the large holes created when Amamet stomped around.

Diana follows her example, landing next to her Aethoes. Both start to walk towards the exit when Artemis hesitates suddenly and quickly turns back to the room, scanning the darkness. Diana pauses with her and looks around, unsure of what is going on. Artemis focuses on a corner and glares into it as if trying to figure out a shape or person within the dark depths. She directs the moonlight to shine upon the corner and finds it empty. Frowning from her discovery, Artemis reluctantly turns and continues to walk towards the exit of the building. Diana glances around a final time and then follows her Aethoes out the Expo dome.

The building doors swoosh open as Diana leaves the scene. She pauses a few feet from the exit and gawks at the number of policemen and security robots that are now pointing their weapons at her. Lawson calls for the Special Forces team to put their weapons down as he approaches and escorts Diana away from the building.

Once they are out of harm's way several of the policemen and robots hurried into the building to secure the scene. Diana notices that all the frat brothers are in handcuffs and unmasked.

Many of them are complaining about a pack of dogs that seemingly disappeared as soon as they exited the building. Diana is only slightly surprised to see that one of the worshipers as the father of the deceased first-night party victim. Raine Pikeys is pacing inside of the police van that she is being restrained in.

"I'm told that you were tied to a strange altar," Lawson says to the intern. "Did they do anything to hurt you?"

"Not that I am aware of," Diana admits. "After we were attacked in the frat house foyer, I fell into a deep hole and hit my head upon the ground when I landed. I was unconscious until my Aethoes woke me up."

"I see," Lawson takes a breath. "However, because of the work that we do, I will be sending you to Tanglewood Hospital to make sure that you are well, per protocol."

"Yes, sir," Diana relents as they arrive at their destination.

"Hmm..." Lawson frowns at the quick agreement. "Deloris, how do you feel now?"

"Much better now that I had a second snack for the night," Deloris answers and holds up her cup. "How did the battle go, Diana?"

"Laurie sacrificed herself and brought Amamet to frightening life," Diana answers and sits down. "Artemis and I defeated the statue. It turned back to stone but fell over and is now destroyed."

"Nako is not going to like that information," Lawson frowns. "What do you have in the robe?"

"It is the Orb of Souls that contain those victims sacrificed over many decades," Diana explains. "It also contains Raquel's soul that we need to return to her body."

"You know the unauthorized taking of evidence from the scene is technically illegal," Lawson explains. "In this case, however, I will overlook it in order to save the life of the young woman."

"Yes sir," Diana stands up. "I'm told we need to get to the hospital quickly."

"Alright," Lawson pulls out a device and pushes a button. "We will all go since you've recently been banned from all buildings on the campus."

"I can explain that," Diana starts.

"No need, I talked to your uncle and he was ok with it," Lawson assures. "Since I am commissioner, they can't ban me from campus. Shall we?"

The hovercar glides over and opens the hatch door to allow passengers inside. Diana climbs in first followed by Lawson. Deloris finishes off her beverage, destroys the cup, then sits down inside the vehicle last. The door closes as the hovercar lifts, turns on its lights, and carefully made its way towards the hospital. It only takes a few minutes of travel to reach the hospital.

The officers exit the vehicle and head straight into the hospital then elevators. Artemis greets her mortal doppelganger on the ICU floor with a nod. Diana smiles wearily at her Aethoes as Lawson goes over to talk to the nurse on duty. She is a colorful representative of the Andromeda Galaxy, complete with webbed fingers and a small fin protruding from her hair.

The nurse listens to the requests of the visitors and scrutinizes their identification. Once satisfied with the documentation, the nurse escorts the P.I.U. officers down the hall towards the requested room. Lawson thanks the nurse as she departs then knocks on the door. The door opens and instead of a relative of the victim, Alys smiles at the detectives then carefully steps into the hall with them.

"Welcome detectives and commissioner," Alys greets quietly. "I am glad you arrived; this family was about to say one last goodbye to their loved one. I asked they hold off for a few more minutes."

"I thought you would be on a hyperplane to Cairo by now," Lawson comments. "Did you miss your flight?"

"Oh, no," Alys waves the concern away. "Nako has a private jet that I am authorized to use so I can leave any time. It was strongly suggested that I stay behind to keep Raquel's body alive long enough for the soul to be reunited. Needless to say, I could not refuse."

"I am glad you are still here, Alys," Diana admits. "Artemis and I figured out how to use the coin. We are not sure how to destroy the orb."

"I'm happy to help," Alys assures. "I will say that Isis and I are pleased that you did not destroy the orb. It is easier to transport the stolen soul."

"We also have the Dagger of Anubis in our possession. Amamet was destroyed," Diana continues.

"That may simply be an illusion," Alys frowns. "We will talk about it later. May I have the orb, please?"

"Of course," Diana carefully unwraps the darkened globe and hands it to Alys. With extreme caution, she rewraps the dagger in the cloth.

"Excellent, please come with me," Alys offers and opens the door to the room to go inside.

"I will stay out here," Deloris volunteers.

"I need to make a couple phone calls, so I'll stay out too," Lawson says and pulls out his phone. He waits until Diana and Alys go into the room and close the door. "Ok, Deloris. What just happened?"

"Do you remember the conversation about Diana and her Aethoes?" Deloris inquires and watches as the man nods. "Same thing applies to Alys."

"Do you predict that we will have more encounters like this as the P.I.U matures?" Lawson asked.

"Not a prediction, almost a guarantee," Deloris assures.

"Lovely," Lawson grumbles. His phone rings prompting him to answer it and walk to the side a little.

Inside of the room, Alys addresses the family of Raquel cheerfully then requests that they leave the room. They start to be resistive but are assured that Raquel is in safe hands. Raquel's mother stands up and leaves followed by the rest of the family. Diana exhales once the door closes, unaware that she is holding her breath. A golden flash in the room heralds Artemis appearance followed quickly by a blue light brightening slowly. Isis smiles at the group in the room as Alys presents the Orb of Souls to her.

The orb starts to pulsate from purple to green as lights within flicker like a flame. Isis lifts the dark orb to eye level and simply taps upon it, causing it to shatter effortlessly. The trapped souls wail happily as they swirl about the room and make their way out of the window. Alys carefully captures Raquel's spirit and gently guides it to the young woman's sleeping body. The spirit and the body once again merge as one and the machines stop working. Several seconds will pass before Raquel is breathing on her own and her eyes flicker open.

"Welcome back, Raquel," Diana says.

"Diana," Raquel greets. "Why didn't you come to the party?"

"I had full intentions of going to the party. However, a few pressing events prevented me from coming that night," Diana says.

"My life depended on your arrival," Raquel informs.

"My attendance at any event should not dictate life or death. You had a choice, you could have used an excuse and left," Diana interrupts as she crosses her arms in annoyance. "Why did you stay and why did you agree to lure me into this trap?"

"I stayed because I was waiting for you," Raquel says as if her feelings are hurt. A moment of silence fills the room.

"And the second part of my question?" Diana coaxes.

"I was there when Laurie sacrificed the girl at the First Night Party and named me her replacement," Raquel explains then turns slightly away. "Laurie told me her plans and, at that time, I thought it was better that you were the next victim than me."

"Raquel, neither of us need be the victim if you had just said something prior to this point," Diana explains.

"Diana, let's depart and let the family greet their loved one," Alys offers, placing a hand on the intern's shoulder.

The door to the room opens on its own as Diana and Alys make their way back into the hall. Before she leaves, Alys gives a warning to Raquel then exits the area. Diana barely gets out of the way as Raquel's family bogart their way back into the hospital room.

Sounds of jubilation echo from the family when they see that Raquel is awake and alert. Diana gathers her thoughts before she informs Lawson and Deloris of Raquel's statements. Deloris scowls and stares at the door as if she could see through it, crossing her arms as she debates if she should enter and question the young woman about the second sorceress from the museum.

A group of security robots lumber down the hall and respectfully request that the group leave the hospital. The unit is now closed to anyone who does not have a family member on the floor. Lawson looks at his watch and frowns. They still had a few hours left for visitors yet the robots insisted, even drawing taser weapons to persuade the group to depart. They retrace their steps and exit the hospital a few minutes later.

"That's not right," Lawson says as he places a stick of gum in his mouth. "Security bots should adhere to the badge of an officer, no matter the branch. Especially college security."

"They have behaved like this since yesterday when Diana and I went to investigate the Expo," Deloris points out. "It does not help that Diana and I are banned from the campus. I believe that was Pikeys's last act before her termination."

"That reminds me," Lawson rubs his scraggly beard as he takes out his remote. "Your ex-professor, Ms. Cummins, has passed away. Prison officials say she died in her sleep. Not sure if I trust that report though."

"My source informs me that she did pass away during slumber. However, she was helped by being smothered by a pillow," Alys says. "Apparently, the lady with the tattoo upon her shin paid an undocumented visit to the late Ms. Cummins."

"La naiba," Deloris swears as she turns to look at the Expo in the distance.

"Is that why Agatha asked us about her sister?" Diana frowns.

"Could be," Alys nods. "It's time for me to depart so I can get back home."

"Like to offer you a ride, Ms. Summers," Lawson says as the hovercar arrives and opens the door. "We zoom past the airport prior to getting downtown anyway."

"Thank you for the offer, Lawson. I accept," Alys smiles. She carefully enters the backseat of the sedan and sits down on one of the couches. Isis joins her, fascinated by the luxurious interior.

"Diana," Lawson addresses as he helped Deloris and the intern into the vehicle. "Your uncle didn't get to tell me what you are going to do for your college years."

"Uncle Julius is a stickler for a higher education," Diana assures as she sits down opposite of her supervisors. "He somehow managed to provide a rare opportunity of attending Dracorn University."

"What?" Lawson frowns as the door starts to close. "How the hell did he pull that off?"

Artemis sits comfortably next to her mortal doppelganger as the car door closes soon after Lawson poses the question. The vehicle rises on a cushion of air and heads towards the exit of the campus. Red lights flash briefly as they cross the border of the parking lot. The on-campus clock tolls the three o'clock hour and the caution tape is up yet all the police have disappeared for the night. Several scenebots comb the interior of the Expo building for all clues related to the case.

The circuitry of the robots starts to short as smoke exits the mechanical bodies and they fall to the ground unmoving. A lone figure steps out of the darkness and levitates up to the floating floor, landing a few feet from the collapsed column. She waves her hand, the motion of which is echoed in the stones that cover both Prof. Murphy and Wyliam. The former teacher is no longer alive, his body crushed to death by the weight of the stones.

The woman simply turns her attention to Wyliam after determining Murphy's fate. She lifts her hand and snaps her fingers. Wyliam bellows in anger as he awakens and frees himself from the rubble, ready for a fight. He turns around several times and then hesitates when he sees the woman standing only feet from him. Instead of attacking, he whimpers and gets down to his hands and knees then ultimately onto his stomach.

The woman places her hand upon her hip as Wyliam grovels over toward her and kisses her feet and ankles, barely missing the tattoo of a ship on the woman's shin. She allows him to do this for several seconds and then simply walks away to stand in front of the area where Laurie last stood. The high priestess's body is no longer there, taken away by the police when they secured the scene.

"Such a damn shame," the woman expresses her disapproval.

Her cape flutters in the breeze slightly as she levitates herself once again and floats down to the main floor in front of the pile of rubble that was once Amamet. Her hands start to glow light green as she lifts them up and draws symbols in the air.

Mystical pictures continue to pulse as she completes her spell and pushes it towards the rubble pile.

The stones click and moan as they meltdown and then consolidate together. The green glow reflects upon the newly formed statue of a thin dark-skinned woman. The statue opens her eyes and rotates her neck as she has new life breathed into her. Her yellow-green eyes focus upon the hooded woman in front of her.

"Who dares to summon me!" Amamet, the dark-skinned woman, demands. Her voice is strong and almost angry.

"You know who I am," the woman says as she lowers her hood. "You have unfinished business, Amamet."

"Yes Mistress," Amamet says and bows.

The new form of Amamet except the robe given to her by the tattooed woman. Wyliam could only gawk as he watches the two head towards the exit of the Expo building. The original woman stops and glances behind her briefly. Wyliam gulps down a little as he jumps, landing on the lower floor in a very ungraceful way. He then scrambles after the two women, careful not to fall behind as he did not want to face the wrath of either of them.

www.ingramcontent.com/pod-product-compliance
Lightning Source LLC
Chambersburg PA
CBHW060304310726
48976CB00007B/2200